D0988989

Cottage on Gooseberry Bay:

A Geek Thing

by

Kathi Daley

This book is a work of fiction. Names, characters, places, and incidents either are products of the author's imagination or are used fictitiously. Any resemblance to actual events or locales or persons, living or dead, is entirely coincidental.

Copyright © 2021 by Katherine Daley

Version 1.0

All rights reserved, including the right of reproduction in whole or in part in any form.

Gooseberry Bay

Halloween Moon

Thanksgiving Past

Gooseberry Christmas

Kiss 'N Tell

Charmed Summer

A Summer Thing

A Geek Thing

Chapter 1

Apparently, finding teenage zombies at the last minute was going to be more difficult than I'd anticipated. Leaning my elbows on my desk, I considered the names I'd crossed off on the piece of letterhead I was staring at, which at one point had provided what I thought would be an adequate list of potential candidates. Boy, was I wrong.

"So, what are we going to do now?" I asked my dogs, Kai and Kallie. I'd promised Hope Masterson a complete list of zombies by the end of the day, and, as of this point, I was still five short of the fifteen I'd promised to recruit.

Kai barked once as if to indicate that he felt my pain and sympathized. When I'd agreed to help Hope recruit volunteers for the upcoming haunted house, I really had thought getting the bodies I'd need would be as simple as making a few phone calls. What I hadn't realized was that the haunted maze and haunted house were being held the same weekend, and, apparently, Shelly Goldblum had jumped on her commitment to finding spooks for the haunted maze and had scooped everyone up before I had the chance to make my inquiries.

Tossing the list aside in a fit of frustration, I tucked a strand of my long blond hair behind an ear and began straightening my desk. I'd been waiting for a potential client who'd called earlier to inquire about my fees for surveillance, but it was already twenty minutes past the time we'd agreed upon, so I wondered if she'd even show. In a way, I hoped she wouldn't. Following someone's husband to prove he was cheating was not the sort of case I usually took on, but when I'd explained that to the woman, she'd insisted on a face-to-face consult just the same. I'd agreed to hear her out, but she was late, and it was well into the afternoon. To be honest, I was motivated to head back to the cottage the dogs and I called home, so I wasn't really interested in waiting around much longer.

Deciding to give the woman ten more minutes, I put my time to good use by watering my one plant, refilling the paper in the copy machine, and locking the file cabinets that lined one wall. After those tasks had been completed, I stepped out onto the sidewalk that bordered Main Street and took in a deep breath of cool crisp fall air. I'd always enjoyed this time of year; the brilliant color, the scent of wood smoke from nearby fireplaces, the crunch of fallen leaves beneath my feet as I walked the forested trails. And, of course, there was the upcoming Halloween event that seemed to bring new energy to the boardwalk. Most of the vendors had strung orange and white lights around their carts or booths, and there wasn't a vendor in sight without at least one bright orange pumpkin to brighten things up.

"Beautiful day," my next-door neighbor said as she stepped out onto the sidewalk.

"It really is," I replied to Edna Jenkins, half owner of Then and Again, the antique shop I shared a wall and a common area with. "It looks like a new vendor is setting up shop across the way."

"The construction is for the ticket booth for the annual Halloween events," she explained. "They set up a booth and sell advance tickets every year. The booth will block your view of the water for a few days, but it's fun to watch all the activity."

"Seems like a lot of work for only a few days," I commented.

She shrugged. "I think the booth goes together pretty easily, and it does tend to draw a crowd, which in turn, provides advertisement."

I guessed that much would be true. I'd rolled into town on Halloween evening last year and really hadn't had the chance to look around at the local offerings. I was excited to be part of the holiday this year, and, despite the trouble that I was having getting the zombies I needed, I was excited to be helping.

I chatted with Edna for a few more minutes and then headed back inside. After the ten minutes that I'd allotted for my potential client to arrive came and went, I grabbed my key, intending to lock the front door. I'd just turned back from my desk to cross the room when two young men, who looked like they might still be in high school, walked in.

"Can I help you?" I asked from my position near my desk.

"Are you Ainsley Holloway?" the taller of the two boys asked while his shorter friend wandered over to say hi to the dogs.

"I am."

"We heard that you find missing people," the shorter of the two said from his squatting position between Kai and Kallie. "Cool dogs, by the way."

I nodded. "I'm a private investigator who does occasionally take on missing persons cases." Actually, since going into business eight months ago, most of my cases had turned out to be missing persons cases, but I felt it was better to present a somewhat wider range to potential clients. "Is someone you know missing?"

The shorter of the two men stood up and walked toward me. "A brilliant physicist named Professor Ivan Beklund."

"I see." I paused and looked a bit more closely at my visitors. "I'm sorry, but I didn't catch your names."

"I'm Skeet, and this here is Ape," the shorter one informed me.

"Skeet and Ape?"

"Those are our Geek Squad names," Ape said.

Geek Squad? I was pretty sure I'd never heard of such an organization. At least not locally. "Is this Geek Squad a club of some sort?"

"A secret society," Ape corrected.

"I see." I didn't. Not really. The tall guy with curly dark hair, huge brown eyes, a lanky body, and overly long arms and legs did look a bit like an ape, but that didn't really explain the rest. I glanced at Ape's shorter counterpart. While the guy did look a bit like a geek with his large wire-rimmed glasses, short hair, and an oversized hoodie, he also appeared to be athletic and muscular beneath his baggy clothing. If he changed his hair and his clothing, he'd probably fit in with the "in" crowd fairly well. Of course, looks weren't everything. Given the fact that the boys were looking for a missing physicist, I supposed I could assume they were smart or at least interested in science. Maybe these smart geeky guys had decided to band together. "Okay, so tell me more about this secret society." I decided to ask. "Is this a school thing?"

"Not a school thing," Ape answered. "A life thing. There are five of us. All intellectually gifted, yet challenged socially. Now can you help us or not?"

"Perhaps," I answered, offering the two boys a seat across from my desk. "Why don't you start by telling me exactly who this Professor Beklund is and why you think he's missing."

They sat down as I'd indicated they should, and then the tall one, who I now knew was referred to as

Ape, began to speak. "Professor Beklund has one of the most brilliant minds in the world, but he's also a loner who, in general, avoids people. At least he avoids people now. I'm not sure if he's always avoided people. I know that he used to work for the university in Seattle, so at one point, he must have gotten along with people okay, but he quit his job and went off the grid about three years ago. Currently, he lives in a cabin in the woods west of here and rarely talks to anyone."

"Anyone other than us," Skeet amended.

"Us as in the two of you?"

"Us as in the Geek Squad," Skeet clarified.

Ape explained. "Professor Beklund is a bit of a geek like us. He gets us. We get him. It just all works out, so he lets us visit. The Saturday before last, the gang went out to the cabin for one of our brain-expanding sessions, but Bek wasn't home."

"So maybe the man was just out for the day when you stopped by," I suggested.

"Maybe. His car was still in the parking area near the trailhead to the cabin, suggesting that he hadn't left the area, but despite our repeated knocking, the guy never answered the door, so we figured that maybe he was out for a hike. It had been a really nice day."

"Okay, that all sounds reasonable. I take it you've been back, and Professor Beklund still wasn't there."

Ape nodded. "Skeet and I went back alone the following day. He still didn't answer the door, although his car was still in the parking area. We started to get worried at this point but didn't take action. Then the five of us all went out to the cabin a third time this past Saturday, and when he still didn't answer, we let ourselves in."

"So you have a key to the cabin?"

"There isn't a key," Skeet answered. "The door is secured with deadbolts that can be unlocked by entering individual codes on a keypad near the door. It's a secure system that isn't easy to break, but Bek gave Apc and me the codes a while back."

"In case of an emergency," Ape added.

"And what did you find after entering the cabin?" I asked.

"Nothing," Skeet answered. "The cabin looks okay. There aren't any signs of a struggle or anything like that, but the guy is just gone."

"And his car is still parked at the trailhead?" I asked.

Both boys nodded.

I paused, not really sure what to do at this point. I could see the boys were concerned, but there were a lot of reasons why an adult might be away from home for a week, and since there hadn't been any signs of a struggle, I didn't see a reason to suspect that foul play was involved. I said as much.

"We get the fact that it appears the guy simply went off somewhere, but there are the threats that should be taken into account," Skeet responded.

"Threats?" I asked. "This professor shared with you the fact that he'd received threats?"

Skeet paused and then answered. "Yes. In a way. Keep in mind that Bek sometimes rambles on and on about things, but he began talking about someone named Evington a couple months ago. I guess he knew Evington from his old life at the university, and apparently, Bek had reason to believe that this man wanted something from him and posed a threat. He never specifically said what Evington wanted, and much of what he said didn't really make sense, but he did keep going on and on about the guy stealing his research and his need to protect it."

"So maybe he left his cabin in the woods in order to protect himself and his work," I suggested.

"Maybe," Skeet admitted. "But we still have a bad feeling about things. Something's just not right. We really want to find the guy just to make sure he's okay."

"Have you notified the police about this missing friend?" I asked.

"We did," Skeet confirmed. "Deputy Todd wouldn't even make the trip out to the cabin to look around. He said the guy might just be on vacation and that unless we had a specific reason to believe the man was in some sort of trouble, he wasn't inclined to get involved. We told Deputy Todd about the threat Bek mentioned, but he just responded that the guy was a nut."

I paused as I tried to figure out what to do next. On the one hand, the theory that the man had met with foul play was a weak one, but on the other hand, if the guy actually was in trouble, I supposed it wouldn't hurt to check it out. "Have either of you spoken to your parents about your concerns?"

"My mom is dead, and my dad is in prison," Skeet said. "My Uncle Trout is my legal guardian, but I haven't seen him for weeks. He likes to gamble and only shows up when he needs a few days to sleep it off. It's cool, though. I'm seventeen, and I can take care of myself."

"And you?" I asked Ape.

"My dad left when I was little, and my mom works a lot. She doesn't have time to help us, and to be honest, even if she did have time, I don't think she would. So what do you think? Will you help us?"

I paused to consider the situation.

"We don't really have any money," Ape added before I could even provide my reply. "But we know how to do things. Maybe if you help us, we can do something for you in trade."

"Something like what?" I asked.

"Our friend, Chip, is really good with computers," Skeet said. "If you need an update or something like that, he'd be the one to help you. And I know how to build things. Robots and stuff." He looked around. "You're a PI. I can help you with a security system, surveillance equipment, drones, tracking devices, and that sort of thing."

I began to speak but then hesitated.

"Please," Skeet persuaded. "We really are concerned about our friend. We know how to do a lot of things, but finding a missing person isn't really in our wheelhouse. I know the gang and I can find a way to pay you back."

I made a decision and answered. "I won't say for certain that I'll take on the case, but I am willing to take the next step and look into things. We can figure out what you can do for me in return later." I realized that the Geek Squad members would round out the number of zombies I needed for the haunted house, but I decided to approach the subject of the volunteer gig after I had a chance to get more information. "I'll need someone to take me out to the cabin where Professor Beklund lives."

"We can take you," Skeet said. "Ape and I. We can go now if you want."

"Okay," I decided. "You said the cabin is isolated. How long will it take to get there?"

"It's about a fifteen-minute drive, and then we'll need to hike in. That usually takes another ten minutes."

I glanced at the dogs, who I knew would welcome a walk. "Do you have your own car?"

Skeet informed me that he did, so I suggested that the dogs and I just follow him.

The drive out to the cabin took us through town and away from the main road onto a service road that was not only rutted and uneven but narrow as well. The road wove through the trees until it eventually ended at a large clearing, where, as the boys indicated it would be, we found an SUV I assumed belonged to Professor Beklund. The boys parked alongside the SUV, so I parked next to them. I let the dogs out of the cargo area of my vehicle, and then the three of us, along with the dogs, took off walking down the narrow trail.

"So, how did you meet Professor Beklund?" I asked as we walked.

"I'm really into a lot of the same things Bek is," Skeet explained. "My main interest is robotics, and I plan to major in engineering, but physics has fascinated me since I was a child. Before Bek decided to go rogue, he published some brilliant ideas, and I've read all his books and papers. Six years ago, I had an opportunity to attend a conference where he was presenting. I was only eleven, but I guess you can say that we hit it off, and we stayed in touch. Then three years ago, the guy just up and quits his job at the university and moves to the cabin in the woods. Since I live in the area, I would visit him sometimes. After a few visits, I introduced him to Ape. Ape is the real physics guy in our group. Even more than me. I knew they'd hit it off, and they did. Eventually, I introduced Chip, Phoenix, and Cosmo to him as well. I'm pretty sure the five of us are the only friends the guy has."

"And you're all in high school?"

"For now," Skeet answered as he began inputting a series of numbers into a keypad near the front door, which apparently opened the seven locks one at a time. "We graduate at the end of this year."

"So the five of you make up the Geek Squad?" I wondered.

Ape jumped in to confirm that was the case as Skeet finished his task and the door popped open.

The cabin was small yet functional. It had no windows, which seemed to be intentional given the man's need for security. There was a single steel door with the seven locks we'd accessed to gain entry. Solar panels stored energy, which operated a small refrigerator and a few lights. There was a real wood fireplace, and the stove was fueled by wood, as was the cleverly constructed heating system. When you took the innovations to the cabin paired with the large garden, greenhouse, well, and water storage system into account, I could see how the man could live totally off the grid, or at least mostly off the grid, for as long as he might desire.

I walked toward the narrow twin bed that was covered with a single green wool blanket. The bed covering reminded me of the blanket my father had owned. He'd shared that the blanket had initially been a standard Army issue that had been given to my grandfather during World War II. I'd never met the man. He'd been dead long before I'd been introduced into the life of the man who raised me. But I did remember that blanket. Dad didn't sleep with it, but he told me that his father had even after he'd returned from the war. It was hot and scratchy, and I couldn't imagine why anyone would choose it for their bed. Still, I supposed when you were sent overseas at a young age to fight a war that you didn't even understand, you took the supplies you were given and never questioned what you had. I also supposed you protected those supplies since you were unlikely to get replacements, so I could understand how an attachment to a scratchy blanket could be formed.

I glanced toward the large desk that sat in the middle of the room and dominated the space so that everything else contained within the area appeared small and insignificant. The desk was not only large but it was cluttered. Stacks upon stacks of folders filled with papers had been randomly scattered across the surface, which also held a computer, books, and notepads.

I'd noticed a short hallway off the main room. I figured there must be a bathroom, although, without a sewer system, there must be a septic tank. When I opened the door, I found a second room that had most likely initially been built to be a bedroom. The room, however, wasn't filled with bedroom furniture; instead, the space was completely filled with rows upon rows of bookshelves, each of them reaching from floor to ceiling and each completely filled with books.

"Wow," I said aloud. "This is really something."

"Bek likes his books."

"I noticed the whiteboards covering most of the walls in the main part of the cabin. Are all those equations Professor Beklund's work?"

Ape nodded. "Bek likes to have a whiteboard handy to work out his ideas when they come to him. Once he works everything out, he transfers the equations to his files, and then he wipes the whiteboards clean for reuse. Most of the stuff on the whiteboards are equations that exist in theory but haven't been worked out yet." Ape looked around the room. "It looks like some of his whiteboards are missing."

"Yeah, I was thinking the same thing," Skeet said.

"Missing?" I asked. "It looks like there are quite a few."

"There are, but there were more at one point," Skeet answered. "I'm surprised I didn't notice the missing whiteboards before."

"Maybe he just stored some away," I said.

Both boys agreed that was likely, but they didn't seem convinced.

"When the Geek Squad came to visit, did you all work on his projects with him?" I asked.

Skeet laughed. "No. All that stuff is beyond us. Most times, Bek would put us to work in the garden. He'd talk to us while we worked. Share a bit about what he had going on."

I walked back into the main room and stood in the center. There was a dining table with four chairs near the tiny kitchen. It also had books and notepads piled atop it. There were dishes in the sink, and the coffee pot on the counter was half full. It didn't necessarily look as if the professor had been abducted. There didn't seem to be signs of a struggle. The room was beyond cluttered, but there seemed to be order to the clutter. If there had been items on the floor, which should have been on tabletops, tipped over whiteboards, or plates with food on them, I might be more apt to buy the abduction theory.

"There isn't anything in this space to indicate to me that the professor you're looking for was forcibly taken from his cabin," I said.

"I admit the space isn't trashed as it might be if a struggle had occurred," Skeet said. "But maybe a struggle didn't happen. What if someone showed up with a gun and the professor decided it would be best to go with them rather than risk being shot?"

"I suppose it could have happened that way," I admitted.

"So, will you help us?" Ape asked.

I paused for just a minute. "I'll help you look into things further," I agreed. "I'll see if I can figure out a way to track the man down. Even though Professor Beklund lived off the grid, he must have had money to buy the food he wasn't able to grow. Fuel for the stove costs money, as does gas and insurance to keep a vehicle."

"The professor has money and a bank account," Ape said. "He mentioned from time to time that he'd invested wisely during his time at the university and had plenty of cash to live the way he chose."

"And a phone?"

Skeet nodded. "Yes. He has a cell phone. He uses it as his primary source of internet, although he does have a satellite as well."

"Okay, then I'll have a starting place. It would help if I had the man's bank records, cell phone number, email accounts, and any other information you might have access to."

"I know his cell phone number, but that's about it," Skeet said.

"We can look for bank information in the file cabinets in the little mudroom off the back of the cabin," Ape suggested.

I hadn't noticed a mudroom when we'd walked through before, but as it turned out, to access it, one had to walk through the cluttered bookroom, making it unnoticeable unless you were looking for it. The file cabinets were locked, but Skeet knew how to break in without damaging the units. The cabinets were stuffed to the point you could barely open and close the drawers, but eventually, I found a file with bank records that gave me account numbers and a place to start. I wasn't sure exactly what sort of information I'd be able to extract from the phone and bank records, but I figured that if those leads didn't tell me anything, the guys and I could always come back.

After making sure the door was securely locked, the dogs, the boys, and I headed back to the cars.

"So about that favor you were going to do for me," I said as we walked along the narrow path.

"Do you need your printer set up, a phone tapped, or someone spied on?" Ape suggested.

"Actually, I need zombies. Five of them."

"Zombies?" Ape stopped walking.

I explained about the haunted house and my job as the volunteer coordinator for the haunted house.

"I see," Ape frowned.

I had to admit that both boys looked confused and just a bit reluctant. Eventually, Ape agreed. "Okay. I'm in." He glanced at Skeet.

"I'm in too," Skeet confirmed. "We'll call Chip, Phoenix, and Cosmo, but I'm sure they'll do it. When do you need us?"

"The haunted house doesn't start until Thursday, but there's a volunteer meeting tomorrow afternoon. It's after school hours, so that won't be a problem. Why don't the five of you meet me at the community center at three-thirty, and I'll bring whatever I've been able to dig up relating to Professor Beklund. If we have a lead to follow, we'll do that after the volunteer meeting. If not, we'll come up with a plan B."

The boys agreed to my plan, so I called Hope to let her know that I'd managed to recruit the number of zombies she needed. I'd been asked to recruit fifteen teenagers in all. I'd already called Hope with the names of the first ten zombie volunteers. When Hope asked me for the names of my last five recruits, I realized I didn't really know their names. I shared their nicknames and promised to provide their real names the following day. Once that was done, the dogs and I headed back to the peninsula where we lived. Now that we had the phone and bank information for Professor Ivan Beklund, I needed to see if my friend and neighbor, Jemma Hawthorn, could use that information to find the clues I'd need to launch my investigation.

Chapter 2

Realizing that I'd left a file I needed back at the office, I decided to stop by on my way home. I parked on the street in front of Ainsley Holloway Investigations, telling the dogs to wait since I'd only be a minute. I hurried into the office through the front door, picked up the file, and was heading back to my SUV when I noticed that my friend, Parker Peterson, was standing on the boardwalk across from my business looking out at the bay. I supposed she might simply be taking a break and enjoying the exceptional view provided by fall leaves and deep blue water, but something about the way she was standing so completely still seemed odd. Making a decision, I told the dogs to wait one more minute while I ran across the busy street that separated the row of mom and pop shops from the vendors lining the wooden walkway.

"Hey, Parker," I said, taking a position next to her.

She turned and smiled at me. "Ainsley. Where'd you come from? I was by earlier, but it appeared that you'd already left for the day."

"I had left, but I needed to come back for a file. Whatcha looking at?"

She glanced out toward a yacht that was sitting perfectly still in the middle of the bay. "See that yacht?"

I indicated that I did.

"I was at the marina maybe two or three hours ago, and I noticed the yacht pull into the harbor. Someone from the yacht boarded a dinghy and ferried over to the wharf. The man from the yacht got out of the dinghy and walked toward the main street running through town. I'm not sure why I even noticed. It's not like it's unheard of for folks touring the area to come ashore and take in the local sights. I was on my way to interview a woman about the bake sale the high school is sponsoring next weekend and continued on my way. Then when I was on my way back through town after finishing work for the day I noticed that the yacht is still there. For some reason, my intuition whispered at me to stop and take note of things."

"I take it something about the whole thing is bothering you."

She frowned. "I don't know. I guess I'm trying to make up my mind about that. On the surface, it doesn't necessarily appear that anything sinister is going on. I just have this feeling that something is going to happen that's going to cause me to look back on this moment and be grateful that I'd taken the time to notice the details. Do you know what I mean?"

"I do. My intuition can be noisy and demanding at times as well. Do you think you're supposed to notice the yacht itself or the man who came ashore?"

She slowly moved her head from side to side. "I'm not sure. Since I've been standing here, I've noticed three men come up onto the deck of the yacht, but the man I saw earlier wasn't one of them. I'm not sure if he's still in town or if he returned to the vessel, but the dinghy is still tied up in the marina. I'm really not sure why I even stopped to watch. The man who came ashore was a pretty normal-looking guy. Dark hair, tall, light blue polo shirt, khaki pants. He looked put together, and the clothes were designer, but I'm not sure if he's the owner of the yacht. He might be, but my sense was that he's an employee of whoever owns the yacht. Maybe he's one of the crew, but more likely a business manager or assistant of some sort."

I smiled. "You were able to pick that all up by simply watching the man come across the bay from the yacht to the wharf in a dinghy and walk toward the street running through town?"

She smiled back. "I've been trained to be observant. The man was dressed nicely, but he didn't have that confident swagger that I suspect the man who owns a yacht the size of this one might possess. He did seem to walk with purpose. As if he had a specific goal in mind and wasn't just window shopping or stopping for a bite to eat."

"You just said you don't know who owns the yacht, so how do you know that the owner would possess a swagger?"

She shrugged. "Just a hunch."

"If you want to walk across the street with me, we can use my computer to see if we can identify the vessel."

She glanced down at her watch and frowned. "Actually, I have a date I'm already going to be late for." She took her cell phone out and snapped a photo. "I can look it up later if my hunch turns out to be accurate and something does happen that will involve that yacht and the man I saw ferry across."

"Okay. If you end up needing help, give me a call me. Have fun tonight."

She grinned. "Oh, I will."

"I take it your date is with someone special."

She lifted a shoulder. "Let's just say the date is with someone with the potential to be special. I guess we'll see if what I'm hoping for is how things work out."

By the time I made it back to the peninsula, dropped my file, computer, and jacket off at my cottage, and the dogs and I headed next door, it was nearly six-thirty. I hoped my neighbor, Jemma, would be home and willing to help me dig around in the life of one very reclusive professor.

"Hey, girl," Josie greeted me when I knocked on the door of the cottage she shared with Jemma. "I hoped you'd stop by. I was actually going to call you."

"You were?" I asked. "What's up?"

Josie stepped aside to allow the dogs and me to enter the cottage just as her cats, Stefan and Damon, came running down the stairs to greet us.

"There's a new waitress at the Rambling Rose," she started by mentioning the bar and grill our mutual friend, Tegan Walker, owned and she worked at. "Her name is Anne. Anne Jorgenson. At least that's the name she goes by, but I sort of think it's an alias."

"Alias?" I asked. "Why would the woman be using an alias?"

"She has that look," Josie explained. She sat down on the sofa before she continued. "She reminds me a lot of Emily."

I knew Emily Brown was a cook at the Rambling Rose who we all suspected to be on the run from someone, although she'd never said anything specific to confirm that.

"So, she dyes her hair, avoids eye contact, and never shares anything about her past."

"Basically," Josie confirmed. "Her hair is black, but the color doesn't match her complexion, so I assume the black has been added to cover her natural color. I've tried chatting with her about places she's worked in the past and things like that, but she basically just gives a vague response like 'down south' and then changes the subject. It's cool. I get it. Sometimes you just need to get gone, and once you're gone, the safest way to stay that way is to disappear. Like I said, she reminds me of Emily. She wants to blend in and not be noticed, but I think her lack of social interaction actually makes her stand out."

"So by avoiding conversations, she's actually drawing attention to herself?"

Josie nodded. "With her detached manner, refusal to speak of her past, and tendency to avoid eye contact, she presents a mystery to solve, and everyone loves a mystery."

"Okay, so what about this woman?" I asked, realizing that we'd veered off topic. "Why did you bring her up in the first place?"

"I think she might be in trouble. Or I think she might potentially be in trouble. I'm not sure of anything at this point, but I have this feeling that things are about to get really bad."

"Get bad? Did something happen?" I asked.

"Sort of," she answered. "I was just merging into the last hours of my shift today when this tall man with dark hair walked in. It was slow, and it was just Anne and me left to cover until the dinner staff arrived, so I agreed to take all three of the occupied tables in the main dining room while she headed to the indoor/outdoor room to clear off a table that had been used by a large group during the lunch hour. Anyway, I don't think the man saw her, but I noticed that she headed out through the back door toward the outdoor patio as soon as she saw him. From there, she left."

"Left the premises?" I clarified.

Josie nodded. "The only explanation I can come up with for her departure is that she saw the guy and freaked. Anne had another hour left on her shift, plus she didn't stop to say anything to anyone or to clock out. She just took off and never came back. I was the only waitress left on shift after she fled, and I had customers, so I couldn't just leave. I gave the man a menu and asked him what he wanted to drink. He ordered coffee. I asked him if he wanted anything to eat with his coffee, but he said he wasn't hungry and the coffee would be fine. He drank it and left."

The behavior exhibited by the man who'd come in seemed totally normal, although Anne's behavior was definitely odd. "Did you try calling Anne?"

"I did," Josie confirmed. "She isn't picking up. When I got off work, I went to the weekly hotel where she'd been living when she first started working for Tegan, but I was told that she'd moved out a couple weeks ago. Tegan and Booker are in Hawaii for another week, but I called Tegan and asked her if Anne had given her a new address, and she said she wasn't even aware that she'd moved. Tegan assured me that she didn't have any contact information for Anne other than the cell phone she carried. She agreed that the woman had a story to tell and most definitely seemed to be running from someone or something, but she also shared that Anne was a hard worker and seemed to really need a job which is why she hired her." Josie took a breath. "I know that it won't be easy to track her down, but I have a bad feeling about things. I hoped that between you and me and Jemma, we could find her and make sure she's okay."

"Where is Jemma?" I asked, looking around the room.

"She had to go to Seattle today for her job, but Coop gave her a lift in his bird, so they should be back at any time. I hoped the three of us could put our heads together and track Anne down. If she is running from this guy and he did find her, she'll likely run again, but if there's any way to help her so she can stop running, I'd really like to try."

"I'll do what I can," I offered. "Do you have anything to go on other than Anne's cell phone number?"

"I pulled her employee file and brought it home with me." She handed me a file. "It won't help, though. It shows Anne's name, age, social security number, cell phone number, and the address at the weekly motel she's already checked out of, but little else. I have a feeling the name and social are fake. I guess Jemma might be able to sort that out once she gets here. During our telephone conversation, I asked Tegan if Anne had said anything that might provide a clue about her actual past when she'd hired her. Tegan said the woman had been very careful and deliberate with her words and hadn't volunteered anything beyond the required information."

"This is a small town," I said. "My initial suggestion would be to just ask around and see if anyone has noticed where Anne moved to, but that might take a while, and if we can track her down that way, then this man who may or may not be after her will be able to do the same. We need to figure out how to find her faster than he can. Does Anne have any friends? Anyone she might have confided in if she actually was in trouble?"

"Maybe Emily," Josie suggested. "I don't know for sure, but I don't suppose it would hurt to ask."

"Does Emily still live above the bar and grill?" I asked.

Josie nodded. "Emily worked the breakfast shift today, so she wasn't there when the man showed up, but she might have an idea of where Anne might have gone off to."

Josie called Jemma, who didn't pick up, so she left a message letting her know what was going on and that she and I were going to see if we could track Emily down and speak to her. Josie asked her to call once she returned to the cottage and said that we'd figure out our next move at that point.

During the drive back into town, I thought about Emily. I knew she'd shown up a couple years ago with her daughter, Ashley, in tow. She approached Tegan about a temp job in the kitchen. Tegan hadn't really needed help with the cooking at that point, but she'd recognized the look of fear in Emily's eyes and the look of hopelessness and fatigue in Ashley's, so she'd not only hired the woman, but she'd given her a place to live as well.

It had been close to a year since I'd met Emily, and in that time, she'd continued to show up for every shift, do her job better than anyone else could, then retire with her daughter to the small apartment above the bar. She didn't seem to have other interests or hobbies, and Ashley didn't go to school, but I suspected that she felt safe staying securely within the self-imposed boundaries of her limited life. Even though I'd never been in a situation where I didn't feel safe, I could imagine that for someone in that situation, feeling safe was probably more important than anything else despite the sacrifices that needed to be made.

As we suspected she would be, Emily was at home with Ashley in her apartment above the Rambling Rose when we arrived. I could sense she was uncertain about inviting us in even though she knew both Josie and me, but after a brief hesitation, she sent Ashley to her room and then stepped aside.

"Thank you for agreeing to speak to us," Josie said after we entered the apartment. "I know you're off work for the day and that Ashley probably has studies to see to, but I'm worried about Anne and hoped you might be able to help us out."

"Anne?" she asked. Apparently, she wasn't aware of Anne's afternoon visitor.

Josie quickly explained about the man who'd come into the bar and grill, Anne's reaction to his arrival, and our desire to help her if she had indeed found herself in a situation where help might be warranted.

"I probably don't know Anne any better than you do," Emily said to Josie. "She's made it clear that she's here to do her job and is uninterested in conversation or friendship. I understand that and have honored her wishes. Our relationship is limited to the hours the two of us work together, and the conversations we have are limited to our customers, the food, and the scheduled work hours for the following week."

"So you have no idea how to get ahold of her?" Josie asked.

Emily hesitated.

"We just want to make sure she's okay," Josie assured her. "She may have left town by this point, but if she hasn't, and if she's hiding out and in need of help, then we want to be there for her."

Emily frowned and didn't answer right away. She seemed to be thinking things over. I suspected that Emily was trying to weigh the pros and cons of helping us find the woman who clearly didn't want to be found. Emily and Josie had worked together since she'd arrived in Gooseberry Bay. I suspected that Emily knew that she could trust her.

"There is a place," she finally said. "Most of the hotels, motels, and rental properties in town require you to have legal ID and a credit card to rent a room, but there is one place that will deal in cash and won't ask too many questions. If Anne had to run and couldn't go home, wherever home might be, and if she wasn't ready or able to leave Gooseberry Bay, she might have gone to this place."

"And where is this place?" Josie asked.

"North of here. Not far. Maybe five miles. Anne doesn't seem to have a car, so I guess she'd either walk or hitchhike if she decided to leave Gooseberry Bay. I doubt she got further than the place I have in mind in the few hours since you last saw her unless she caught a ride with someone heading north along the main highway leading toward Port Townsend."

"Are you willing to give us the name of the place?" Josie asked. "Maybe directions too."

After more consideration, Emily agreed.

Chapter 3

It was while we were on our way to the dive motel Emily had told us about that Jemma called to let us know she was home. Josie caught her up while I drove, and Jemma assured us she'd be waiting at the cottage for our return.

While the motel had been a good guess on Emily's part, Anne wasn't there. She'd turned her cell phone off by this point, and we really had nothing else to go on, so Josie and I decided to head back to the cottage. We chatted about the situation with Jemma, who agreed that we really couldn't do anything to help Anne without something more to go on. I thought about my promise to the Geek Squad. So I filled the roommates in on the mystery of the missing professor once the three of us were settled on the sofa in front of the fire with a fruit and cheese platter.

"Are you sure the guy isn't just out of town?" Jemma asked. "I understand why the boys you spoke to might have reason to believe the man is acting out of character, but I sort of hate to go digging around in the guy's life if he isn't in trouble."

"I'm not sure of anything at this point," I admitted. "But based on what I observed while touring Beklund's home this afternoon, the professor is extremely protective of his work, and if the guy really is as reclusive as the boys indicated, I suppose it's unlikcly that he simply went somewhere. I thought we could start by looking at phone records and take it from there. If we look at his phone records and can track him down without going any further, I'll at least be able to assure the guys that the professor is okay."

Jemma shrugged. "Okay. I'm in. Do you have a number?"

"I do." I handed Jemma the piece of paper I'd jotted the professor's cell phone number down on.

She got up and headed upstairs to grab her laptop while Josie headed into the kitchen to figure out something to make for dinner. Jemma was good at what she did, and she'd hacked into phone records of others in the past, so I knew it would likely only take her a few minutes. I pulled my cell phone out to see that I'd a missed call from my good friend, Adam Winchester. He hadn't left a message, so I doubted it was important and decided to wait and call him after I returned to my cottage for the day.

"Okay, I'm in," Jemma said. "The guy doesn't make or receive a lot of calls. In fact, there are entire months when no calls are made or received."

"The guys did say that the professor mainly uses his cell phone for the internet. What was the last call he made or received?"

"There are three calls from a local number made to his cell phone in the past week and a call from the same number made to the cell phone four weeks ago. The three recent calls look to have been unanswered and diverted to voicemail, and the call four weeks ago lasted only one minute. There's also one three months ago that lasted five minutes. Hang on, and I'll trace the number back to its source."

I waited while Jemma searched. Again, it only took a couple minutes.

"The phone belongs to Max Hamilton," Jemma said.

"Can you figure out who this Max Hamilton is?"

"Yeah, hang on a sec." She continued to type. "Maxwell Hamilton is a high school student currently attending Gooseberry High." She turned the laptop around so I could see the image on the screen.

"That's Skeet," I confirmed. "He's one of the two boys who hired me to find the missing professor. I guess it makes sense that he's been calling him. Is that it? No other calls either to or from the professor's cell phone?"

"Not in the past three months. I can go back further."

"No." I sighed. "That's probably not necessary. Is the cell phone on now?"

Jemma rolled her lips. "I'm not sure. Hang on, and I'll see if I can ping it."

This took a while longer, and by the time Jemma was able to confirm that the cell phone was turned off, disabled, or destroyed, Josie had dinner ready. Tonight she'd made tacos with some of the pulled pork she had left from the sandwiches she'd made a couple nights ago. I really wasn't sure why Josie wanted to come home and cook after working in a bar and grill all day, but she said that it relaxed her and that after working at the Rambling Rose all day, she wasn't really all that into going out to eat at the end of the day. I supposed that I should just be grateful that Josie found relaxation in the kitchen since I was invited to enjoy the fruits of her labor quite often. Tonight Josie not only made the pulled pork tacos, but she'd made guacamole, homemade salsa, and black beans as well.

"So the phone records didn't help us. What do you want to do now?" Jemma asked me after we'd made our plates and sat down at the dining table to eat the food Josie had whipped up.

"I'm not sure. I guess we can check bank records, but I don't anticipate learning anything from them if the man has been kidnapped. Of course, if he just took off, then we'd know if he's been withdrawing cash from his account, or if he withdrew a large amount just before his disappearance, that might tell us something as well." I took a bite of my taco and chewed slowly. "I suppose it might be worthwhile to see if we can find anything on Evington. I don't have a first name or any other information to go on. Actually, maybe Evington is the first name, and we're short a last name. Still, a search might turn up something. If the man is after Beklund's work, then he must be involved in some sort of profession where physics would come into play." I paused. "Or at least mathematics. I remember the boys mentioning that the professor told them that he needed to protect his equations."

"Maybe running a background check on Ivan Beklund would be beneficial," Josie suggested. "If we know who he is and where he came from, that might give us additional avenues of investigation."

I nodded. "I'll grab my laptop and start on that while Jemma looks into the bank records. I don't have her hacking skills, but I'm pretty good at doing a deep search."

Josie did the dishes and then started baking a batch of brownies while Jemma and I worked at the table. I still didn't know if the guy was even in trouble, but I had promised the Geek Squad that I'd take a look, and I really did want to have something to report to them when we met at the volunteer meeting the following day. Even if the only thing I had to report was that I'd followed several avenues and had come up empty, at least that would demonstrate that I was taking their request seriously and really had tried.

"Nothing here," Jemma said after several minutes. "The guy has a couple hundred grand in this account and only spends around two grand a month. His withdrawals are usually for a grand at a time, and the last withdrawal he made was three weeks ago. Nothing larger than usual and no withdrawals just before or after his disappearance." She looked up at me. "Any luck on your end?"

"Not really. Ivan Beklund was born on August eighth, nineteen fifty-six, which would make him sixty-five. He has two doctorates, one in mathematics and one in theoretical physics. He was a professor at UCLA before he decided to go overseas, where he worked at the University of Edinburg in Scotland for a decade. He most recently taught at the University of Washington before retiring three years ago. As the boys indicated, he seems to have gone off the grid at this point. I found a long list of publications, both books and journal articles. It really does look as if the guy was a big name in his field at one point."

"Ever married?" Josie asked.

"Not as far as I can tell," I answered. "It looks like the professor traveled widely. There are mentions of conferences he spoke at all over the world. I suspect he was one of those academics who was married to his research."

"Any mention of anyone named Evington?" Josie asked.

"Not that I've seen so far. I'll keep looking."

"I'll look too," Jemma offered.

Josie took the brownies out of the oven to cool. She picked up her cat, Stefan, and curled up on the sofa. The cottage smelled like chocolate and nuts, and even though I was still full from dinner, my mouth was watering. Maybe I'd splurge and have one before I left. With a cup of Josie's excellent coffee, of course. The roommates had done a great job decorating their cottage for the fall season and Halloween. The orange lights and tall black candles on the mantel provided a Halloween feel, while the white lights strung over the back deck gave off a warm and cozy vibe. I knew that Jemma had tried hanging garland in a few key locations, but the cats wouldn't leave it alone, so she eventually just took it down. She'd offered it to me, so maybe I'd take her up on her offer and decorate my mantle.

"I found a man named Ronald Evington who taught at UCLA at the same time Beklund was there," Jemma said after a few minutes of searching. "He quit and left academia for the private sector shortly after Beklund left for Scotland. He currently owns a research facility specializing in artificial intelligence, which just so happens to be located in Seattle."

"Interesting," I said. "Both men started off in LA and ended up in Seattle even though they took different paths. That must mean something."

"Maybe," Jemma agreed. "Or it could just be a coincidence. I'll keep digging around. Maybe I can dig up something specific that might hint at the reason behind Evington's desire for the equations that Beklund mentioned to the boys Evington might have wanted. Even if we can figure out what sort of equations Beklund was referring to, that isn't going to prove that Evington has him or that he's even been kidnapped."

"Yeah. I think this case is going to be a tough one to make much progress on unless we can find something more to work with. But I told the boys I'd try, so I will." I stood up. "I guess I should get going. I need to walk the dogs, and I still have some work to do tonight. Since I have a full day tomorrow, I should try to get a good night's sleep, so I'll be ready for an early start in the morning."

"Will you be at the volunteer meeting tomorrow?" Jemma asked.

"I'll be there with my fifteen zombie volunteers. How'd you do with the props?"

"All lined up," Jemma confirmed.

I looked at Josie. "And the food vendors?"

"We're good to go," she confirmed.

"Wonderful." I slipped my laptop into my computer bag. "I've never been the sort to get involved in community events, but I find that I'm enjoying being part of things now that I'm living here in Gooseberry Bay."

"It feels good to give back," Josie said. "Jemma and I have been helping out for years, and of course, Hope dedicates a significant amount of her time to various projects."

"Hope seems to have more energy than your average person," I stated. "And she's really organized. She seems to know exactly what to do and when to do it."

"She's been volunteering for a lot of years," Jemma said. "I guess she's worked out the flow. She reminds me of my new client. Janel is a twenty-eight-year-old owner of a very successful business that helps young professionals and those in the public eye develop and maintain a public image that is both unique and alluring. She tells them how to dress, where to eat, who to date, and sometimes even where to live. She helps individuals with natural talent in a specific area get noticed."

"That sounds interesting," I said.

"It is sort of interesting. It's amazing to me that wearing the right shoes and driving the right car can make a difference in whether a talented singer, attorney, or real estate agent will live out their life on the sidelines or if they'll get noticed and make it big. Don't get me wrong, the talent has to be there, and if it is, Janel can help you make little changes which she assures me will get you the recognition you need to prove yourself."

Josie laughed. "You know I love you, Jemma, but if this woman is into the whole personal style and public image thing, I'm sort of surprised she hired you to help with her database."

Jemma smiled. "Yeah, I was surprised as well since we all know that I'm a jeans and no makeup sort of gal who, more often than not, has cat hair all over my blouse. But one of my other clients recommended me to Janel, and we actually worked everything out through email before I even met her. I've only met with her in person twice, and I did try to leave the cat hair at home but based on the photos of her clients lining her walls, I'm not even in the same league as the individuals she works with."

Josie looked down at her jean-clad frame. "I wonder what she'd recommend for me."

"If you're asking what she'd recommend for Josie Wellington, the waitress, probably comfortable shoes. But if you ever decide to open your own restaurant or write a cookbook, I guarantee she'd have some pretty specific suggestions based on your goals, budget, looks, and personality."

I picked up my computer bag and glanced at the dogs giving them a look that let them know I was ready to head out. "While this conversation has been fascinating and actually has me wondering what Janel would recommend for me, I have a file to go over and a report to write for a client, so I really do need to get going. I guess I'll talk to both of you at the volunteer meeting tomorrow."

"We'll be there," Jemma said. "Cat hair and all."

Chapter 4

"Talk about the perfect autumn day," I said to Kai and Kallie as we walked through the forested section of the bluff trail that we hiked or ran almost every day. The sun was high in the sky, yet the air felt crisp, even cool in the shade. The leaves on the vine maples that wound their way beneath the canopy of pines were painted in varying shades of red, orange, or yellow, depending on the amount of sunlight each shrub enjoyed. The ferns growing along the little river, which by this point in the year was barely more than a trickle, had begun to fade as the days grew shorter and the nights had become colder.

Pausing briefly to take in this moment's perfection, I closed my eyes and listened to the sounds of the breeze rustling through the trees. The aspens quaked, creating a melodic song complementing the babbling water of the nearby brook as it made its way between rocks cluttered with fallen leaves. I took in a deep breath of cool fall air as the songbirds perched in the trees overhead prepared for their morning meal. I loved all the seasons and was apt to embrace each as it ebbed and flowed, but if I had to choose a favorite, autumn would be my choice every time.

After a moment of silent contemplation on my part, I continued down the path toward the back fence of the Winchester Estate. I'd tried calling Adam the previous evening, but he hadn't picked up. I supposed I should have left a message, but I hadn't. I'd reasoned that if the missed call from him the previous day had been important, he would have left a message. Since he hadn't, I could only assume that his call had been friendly in nature and not one intended to impart information or ask a question.

Adam's brother, Archie, was out of town. He'd been away for quite a while, and I suspected that Adam grew lonely at times rambling around in that big old house with only his housekeeper, Ruth, and gardener, Moses, for company. I knew that Adam had been busy as he revamped the foundation left to him and Archie by their parents when they died. I also knew that being busy wasn't always a cure for loneliness, a state of being I'd experienced a time or two after my father died but before I'd moved to Gooseberry Bay.

Adam was a hard worker and was often busy. I knew he'd had to work twice as hard since his brother had never taken much interest in the charitable endeavor. Adam never complained, but I knew he wished Archie would take more interest in the legacy left to both of them when their parents died.

As we climbed the trail, the dogs and I paused several times to take in the view as well as the fresh morning air. There were places along the path where the trees cleared, presenting breathtaking views of the bay far below the bluff. Most days, I ran the five-mile round trip to and from the fence where we usually turned around, but today, I felt motivated to simply meander.

By the time the dogs and I made it back to the cottage, it was well into the morning. I guessed the early start I'd planned to make wasn't going to happen. I gave the dogs food and fresh water, took a shower and dressed, and then grabbed an apple for the road. Usually, I took the dogs with me when I went into the office, but I had the volunteer meeting, and my schedule was uncertain today, so I decided to leave them at home where they'd probably sleep until I got home in the afternoon. Of course, there was a good possibility that Jemma would take them to her cottage to play with the kittens as she often did on the days I left them behind.

Before I left for town, I checked my cell phone and text messages. There was one message from Josie letting me know that Anne had shown up for work today and hadn't said a thing about just disappearing the previous afternoon. When Josie had asked her about it, she said she'd felt sick and needed to go. She hadn't offered any additional information to support her story, and she'd made it clear that she really didn't want to talk about it. It seemed obvious that Anne had been spooked by the man who'd come in. It seemed equally obvious that she must have had a reason to believe he'd moved on since she hadn't left town or continued to avoid the Rambling Rose.

I was glad that Anne was back, but I thought it was odd that she'd be freaked out enough to run but then return the following day to the very place she'd seen the man less than twenty-four hours earlier. I supposed she might have watched him leave and felt safe to return to work, but how could she be quite that certain he wouldn't come back? I didn't know Anne's story and doubted I ever would. Most folks who were on the run didn't trust anyone, and most times, their lack of trust, came with a darn good reason.

As I drove toward my office, I found myself wishing I'd been able to dig up more on Professor Beklund and the status of his current whereabouts. I really didn't know anything more now than what the boys from the Geek Squad had already told me. I knew that sometimes uncovering the truth took time, but assuming the Geek Squad guys were correct in their assumption that the man had been kidnapped, he could very well be alive and waiting to be rescued. It was only eleven a.m. now, and I wasn't going to meet the Geek Squad members until three, so I supposed I had a few hours to figure out something more.

When I arrived at my office across from the boardwalk, I looked out over the bay and noticed that the yacht that had been anchored there yesterday was gone. I wondered if Parker had learned anything about it but decided she probably hadn't. I hung my light jacket on a peg near the door, booted up my computer, checked the messages on my landline, and called Adam one more time. I supposed that if he didn't answer this time, I'd leave a message.

"Ainsley," he said after picking up. "I'm glad you called back. I noticed a missed call from you this morning, but I was in a meeting and decided to catch up with you once I got home."

"And are you home?" I asked. "Should I call back at another time?"

"I'm home. In fact, I just arrived. Are you at the cottage?"

"No, I'm in town. At my office, to be more specific. I have the volunteer meeting this afternoon, but I figured I'd do some work between now and then. The reason I called was because I noticed a missed call from you yesterday."

"Yes. I had a few minutes and wanted to ask you about tonight, but I figured it could wait, so I didn't leave a message. I intended to call you back, but then an old friend stopped by, and I lost track of time. I guess my decision not to leave a message resulted in an unnecessary round of phone tag."

"Tonight?" I asked. "You wanted to ask me something about tonight?"

"I did," he confirmed. "I figured we were both planning to attend the volunteer meeting, so I thought that perhaps we could plan to have dinner after. It'll be early, but maybe we can pick up some steaks and grill them at your place."

"I'd like that." I thought about Skeet and Ape. "I have some new clients who I may need to spend some time with after the meeting. Nothing has been decided at this point, but it is a possibility. Maybe we can settle our dinner plans after I've had a chance to see how everything works out."

"That's fine. I'll be at the volunteer meeting either way. We can talk there."

"Sounds good." I thought about the missing physicist. "Listen, before you go, I wanted to ask if you know a man named Ivan Beklund. He's a retired physicist who's currently living in the area."

"Sure, I know Beklund. He lives in a cabin in the woods outside of town. Brilliant man. A bit eccentric but brilliant. Why do you ask?"

"I guess he's missing. In fact, finding him is the case I referred to earlier."

"Missing?" Adam gasped. "What do you mean missing?"

"The boys who hired me are certain that he's been kidnapped. I'm less certain of that, but the boys are worried that they haven't seen or heard from him in the past week. I'm just starting my investigation, so I don't know much at this point."

"Who hired you to find Beklund?"

"A couple teenage boys who claim to be representing a group known as the Geek Squad. We negotiated a trade. I needed zombies for the haunted house, and they wanted to find their friend, so I agreed to help them if they agreed to help me. I don't suppose you might know anything about where the man might be? If he hasn't been kidnapped, that is."

"No," Adam answered. "Bek doesn't get out much. He mostly stays holed up in his cabin, working on theoretical equations that most likely won't be solved in his lifetime. Have you been to the cabin? Looked around?"

I confirmed that I had and then briefly shared what I'd found. There hadn't been any evidence of a struggle, but just because the kidnappers didn't leave evidence behind didn't mean the man hadn't been kidnapped. "So, how exactly do you know this man?" I asked.

Adam paused and then answered. "I'm interested in education, as you know, and Bek's an educator, or at least he was before his move from Seattle to Gooseberry Bay. Over the last decade, I've spoken with a handful of educators, particularly those from local universities, about my ideas. I know I'm just now getting around to making the changes I've wanted to make within the foundation, but I've been noodling on the idea of refocusing on education and maybe even opening a school for gifted teens for years. Professor Beklund is one of many professors I spoke to while doing my research, and I have to say he was one of the most interesting."

"Have you been out to his cabin?" I asked.

"A time or two. Bek likes expensive scotch, and I can afford to bring him expensive scotch. I'll bring a bottle, and we'll chat. Sometimes I'll ask for his input about some of my ideas. There's no denying that the man is eccentric, but the man is also brilliant. More than that, he seems to really like kids. Intelligent teens, that is. He has a soft spot for them, which is why I value his opinion when it comes to my plans for my school for gifted teens."

"So it fits for you that he'd befriend five intellectually gifted but socially challenged teenagers?"

"Absolutely. Bek has a problem with most adults. but, like I said, he has a soft spot for intelligent teens."

I supposed that made me feel somewhat better about things. At least I now knew that the members of the Geek Squad probably did hang out with the missing professor and probably knew and understood his routines better than most.

"You said you may be meeting with these kids after the volunteer meeting," Adam continued.

"Yes. I spoke to them yesterday, and we agreed that we'd meet after the volunteer meeting. If I had news to share, I would share it then, and if I hit a dead end, which I have, we'd discuss that as well. Maybe come up with a plan B."

"Would you mind if I came along with you when you met with the boys?" Adam asked.

"Not at all. At this point, I could use all the ideas and input I can get. I'm having a hard time even getting started with this one."

"Okay. Then I'll see you at the meeting at three, and we'll talk afterward. I probably don't know Bek as well as the kids do, but I might have a different perspective to offer. If I can help, I'd like to."

"Great. I'll see you then."

After I hung up with Adam, I pulled up Ronald Evington on the computer. I'd thought things through a bit and decided that because of an undefined motive and nonexistent suspect list, all I could really do was start with the one name I had. If that didn't pan out, then maybe while researching my one lead, other names would come to the forefront, and I'd pick up a suspect or two to consider.

As we'd discovered the previous evening, Ronald Evington had taught at UCLA at the same time Beklund was there, although Evington eventually quit and left academia for the private sector. I knew he currently owned a company called Intelligene, a research facility specializing in artificial intelligence. Intelligene was based in Seattle, although an exhaustive search uncovered facilities in seven other states. I supposed if Evington's company was messing around with artificial intelligence and Beklund had information that would blow the lid off the current limitations and parameters of that sort of thing, that information would be invaluable to someone like his former colleague. I could understand how someone with God-given intelligence like Beklund might take exception to the idea of intelligence that was born through a computer and not in the human brain. I could also understand how an approach such as that might cause him to want to keep the information he had to himself. Beklund seemed to have adequate money for his lifestyle, so he probably wasn't going to be swayed by the promise of a big payday. If Evington was desperate for the math that Beklund had worked out, and he knew bribery wouldn't work, might he have resorted to violence?

I really didn't know enough about any of this to know if this sort of logic even made sense, but given the fact that, according to the boys, Beklund had specifically mentioned Evington by name, it seemed as good a place as any to start my investigation. I'd barely gotten started, however, when Parker breezed into my office through the front door.

"Somctimes I amaze myself," she said, sitting down on one of the chairs across the desk from me.

"Amaze yourself?"

She nodded. "Remember when you ran into me across the street yesterday? I was watching the yacht that had anchored in the bay."

"Yes, I remember."

"And remember I told you I had a hunch that something about the yacht or the man who ferried over from the yacht was going to end up being important at some point?"

"Yes, I remember that as well."

"Well, I hate to sound so self-satisfied when a man is dead, but it turns out that I was right."

"Dead?" I gasped. "You said a man was dead. Who?"

"Braylon Dario. The tall man with dark hair wearing the light blue polo shirt and khaki pants I saw come ashore from the yacht yesterday."

I frowned. "How do you know he's dead?"

"We received an anonymous tip at the newspaper. I went to check it out and found the man lying face down in a forested area hugging the edge of the bay. He'd been shot in the back, although it looked as if he'd been shot elsewhere. The body was wet, so my guess is that the guy was shot and then dumped in the bay before he washed up on the shore where I found him."

"Wow." I frowned. "Any suspects?"

"No," Parker answered. "I've just begun my investigation, and Deputy Todd is being closed-lipped as usual. I have a contact in the coroner's office who confirmed that the man died yesterday, probably between six and eight p.m. While his clothing was wet, he didn't have water in his lungs. As I've already indicated, the cause of death was a single gunshot wound to the back and not drowning."

"Wow," I said once again, sitting back in my chair. "I have to hand it to you; your instinct was spot on. What do you know about the man?"

Parker leaned forward slightly. "Not a lot," she admitted. "Like I said, I'm just getting started with my investigation." She placed her hands on the armrests of the chair and stood up. "Listen, I need to run. I talked my friend at the coroner's office into letting me look at the body, but she wants me to come by while her boss is at lunch, which, according to her calculations, should be in about twenty minutes. I doubt I'll make it to the volunteer meeting, but if I find out anything interesting, I'll call you." With that, Parker breezed out the door as briskly as she'd breezed in.

Chapter 5

The volunteer meeting I'd planned to attend that afternoon was geared toward all volunteers assigned to any task relating to the haunted house, haunted maze, and Halloween Festival. I expected to see quite a few people, but I really hadn't anticipated that nearly half the residents of Gooseberry Bay would be there. It took me a few minutes to locate the Geek Squad, who I'd planned to catch up with during the meeting, but I eventually noticed Ape's head towering above the rest of the crowd and headed in that direction.

"We wondered what happened to you," Ape said.

"I've been here for a while, but I had a hard time finding you all in the crowd." I turned to look toward Skeet, who was standing next to a pixie of a girl with thick, dark curly hair.

"This here is Phoenix," Ape introduced the girl. "Behind her is Cosmo and Chip."

"I'm happy to meet you all," I said to the group, focusing in on Cosmo with his longish blond hair, stout body shape, and dark brown eyes, and Chip, with his mop of red hair, green eyes, a smattering of freckles, and lanky frame.

"Do you have news for us?" Ape asked, a tone of anxiety in his voice.

"Not a lot but some, I suppose. Let's listen to what Hope has to say, and then the six of us, along with my friend, Adam Winchester, will head over to my office for a nice long chat."

The five members of the Geek Squad all agreed to my plan. I could sense their impatience to get on with our meeting, but they paid close attention to what Hope shared, signed the forms she passed out, agreed to shifts, and verified their willingness to show up for those shifts dressed per the recommendations.

Once all that was done, the Geek Squad, Adam, and I headed to Ainsley Holloway Investigations to come up with a plan to track Professor Beklund down. It was still somewhat unclear to me whether or not the man was actually in need of rescue or if he'd simply gone off to attend to whatever might need to be taken care of, but in cases such as this where the facts were unclear, I found it best to err on the side of caution.

I started the meeting by introducing Adam to the members of the Geek Squad. They all knew who he was, most everyone living in or near Gooseberry Bay did, but he didn't know them, and I really hadn't had a chance to speak to Chip, Phoenix, or Cosmo, so we took a few minutes to get acquainted. Once that had been accomplished, Adam jumped right in by asking what, if anything, the kids knew about what Bek had been working on at the time of his disappearance.

"Bek always has a lot of different things going on," Skeet said. "He has a brilliant mind, but his thoughts aren't always all that organized."

"Yeah," Chip agreed. "He'd be telling us about the progress he was making on one of the dozen or so equations he was trying to work out, and then he'd segue into a discussion of hothouse tomatoes and the specific nutrient needs required to make them grow to the size of a cantaloupe."

"He seemed mostly interested in work he was doing relating to a project he'd been involved in at some point in the past," Ape said. "As Skeet and Chip mentioned, at times his rambling was difficult to follow, but the last time we spoke, he mentioned that he'd finally been able to work out the math for a project he'd been involved in more than two decades ago."

"Did he specify the type of project he'd been working on?" Adam asked.

"Not really," Ape answered. "I asked if it had anything to do with string theory or dark matter, two areas of interest to me, but he said the project he'd been trying to work out the math for had originated with some work he'd done in neurobiology."

"Bek is a physicist first and foremost, but he dabbles in a lot of different areas," Cosmo explained. "He knows more about astronomy than I do, which is saying a lot since the stars are my classroom and the universe my goal."

Adam was quiet. It appeared he was thinking things through. Finally, he spoke. "Ainsley told me that you mentioned that Bek made a comment about keeping something away from Evington."

Ape nodded. "He didn't say what exactly, but he said he figured something out that would be important to Evington and that he needed to protect his equations."

"Evington works with artificial intelligence," I pointed out. "Bek seemed to be working on a project based in the field of neurobiology which is the field that studies the brain. Maybe whatever he figured out was something that could be extrapolated and used to make improvements in intelligence related to the artificial kind."

"That actually makes sense," Phoenix volunteered. "I know one of the things he was working on had to do with isolating the thought from the action. There's been a lot of work done in this area already, but Bek seemed to think there was something more to find. I know he was not only interested in the sequence but in the timing of the sequence. Bek wanted to know if an intended action differed in sequence and timing from seemingly random or spontaneous behavior. And then, of course, there are automatic behaviors such as taking a breath.

If the exact sequence and the mechanics involved can be isolated and predicted, could it be duplicated?"

"We're all pretty smart," Ape said. "Hence the geek label, but the stuff Bek was working on was way beyond anything any of us can really understand. He'd talk to us about ideas, and he'd voice questions and concepts. Some of it made sense, and some of it didn't. It was still interesting to listen to even if we couldn't really understand what he was trying to do."

"I suppose we could find someone who would understand and ask them to look at the whiteboards Bek has in his cabin," I suggested.

"No," Skeet said. "Bek wouldn't like that. He's very protective of his work. The equations on those whiteboards are his babies. Even if he was in trouble of some sort, he wouldn't want anyone disturbing his work."

Adam spoke. "I don't suppose it's all that important to really understand what he was working on. We just need to figure out where he went off to."

"There was no sign of a struggle in the cabin, and his cell phone shows calls from Skeet, but no other calls to or from the man in the past few months," I said. "His bank records are clean as well. To be honest, I'm not really sure where to go from here."

"How about surveillance cameras?" Adam asked. "I've been out to the cabin. I know the level of security in place. It doesn't make sense that Bek would install all that and not have cameras and an alarm so that he knows in advance if someone is coming."

"Yeah," I said. "That does make sense. If it was me, I'd have added an alarm and cameras in the woods so that I'd know if I had a visitor before they even reached the cabin."

"He never said that he had anything like that, but now that you mention it, he did always seem to know when we were coming. Most of the time, as we rounded the corner and the cabin came into view, he'd be waiting for us on the front deck," Ape confirmed.

"I never noticed cameras or screens," Chip said.

"They're probably hidden," Phoenix pointed out. "You know how paranoid the guy is."

"If the security system recorded the video feed, we might be able to see exactly when Bek left the property and who, if anyone, he left with," Cosmo said.

"Most systems like the one you mentioned have very limited, if any, memory," Skeet pointed out. "The alarm and cameras are intended to provide eyes on the perimeter in real-time. I doubt it would do any good to go looking for them."

"Skeet might be right about there not being recordings to observe, but I don't suppose it would hurt to go out to the cabin and look around," Phoenix suggested.

We all agreed that looking for an early alarm system might be a worthwhile endeavor, so Adam and I took his car and followed Skeet and the other

Geek Squad members out to Professor Beklund's place.

"It looks like you've stumbled onto a pretty complex case," Adam said to me as we drove toward the property the professor owned.

"I'm having a hard time deciding if there's even a case to solve. I'd never even heard of the guy before Skeet and Ape came to talk to me yesterday, so I will admit I don't have a feel for how the man might or might not act, but there really isn't anything to suggest that the guy didn't simply leave on his own accord."

"Bek isn't the sort to simply head out on vacation, nor does he seem to have ties to the outside world," Adam said. "He's never mentioned family, and as far as I know, he never married nor had children. Bek really isn't the sort to have established friendships, and while he used to do the conference tour, I'm fairly certain he's been out of academia in any sort of public way for quite some time. Still, he is an intelligent man with a strong paranoia in place. It seems unlikely to me that someone would have been able to sneak up on him and take him from his home without his permission. At least not without doing considerable damage to the property, which according to what you've said, isn't at all evident."

"The place appeared to be locked up securely, and while it was cluttered, I was assured that not so much as a piece of paper was out of place when the boys took me there yesterday."

"I guess we'll see if there's a video surveillance system set up as we suspect. If there is and the system recorded any activity, that might tell us more than we know now."

I glanced out the window at the tall pines, colorful maples and aspens, and browning ferns as we turned off the main road onto the dirt road leading out to the parking area. The little bridge that crossed the now shallow fall creek caused Adam's SUV to dip and sway as we made our way across. I wondered if Professor Beklund was ever lonely living way out here on his own. I liked the quiet at times, and I supposed most people did, as well, but not only did the man not have neighbors, he didn't even have a dog. I thought about Kai and Kallie and how much they'd helped me struggle through the changes after the man who'd raised me died. I thought about my tendency to think of my dad as the man who'd raised me now that I knew my biological mother and father died in a plane crash when I'd only been three years old.

Adam made a comment about rain being in the forecast as he parked in the same clearing where we'd parked yesterday. He also commented about needing to stock up on wood for the winter and that he'd be happy to help me stock a sufficient supply to get me through the long cold nights ahead. As we walked, Adam chatted with the Geek Squad about school and their plans for the future. He told them about his plans for a school geared toward gifted teens who didn't quite fit into other private ventures, and all five teens voiced their opinion that something like that would have been a Godsend for them had the option been available.

As we neared the cabin, we all looked up rather than ahead. If there were hidden cameras and no one had noticed them before, chances were they were located in the trees and camouflaged by the evergreen branches.

"There," Ape said, pointing upward. He looked at Adam with genuine respect. "You were right. I don't know why it never occurred to me to look for cameras. I mean, that sort of thing is right up my alley."

Phoenix walked across the clearing and approached another grouping of trees along the perimeter. "There's another one here."

The kids found three more cameras along the way, which Ape assured us were most likely attached to a motion sensor and tied into an alarm of some sort. We continued toward the cabin that looked just the same as it had the previous day. As he had yesterday, Skeet entered the codes to each of the seven locks. We all filed in to find the interior of the cabin as undisturbed as it had been. A quick look around netted us the information that the television on the wall doubled as a screen for the external cameras. All five kids admitted that they'd noticed the screen but just assumed the professor liked to watch movies in the evenings or perhaps DVDs of conferences he'd attended.

We looked around the main living area extensively and didn't find any sort of recording device, but Ape suggested we take a closer look in the library or file room. It made sense that if recording equipment existed, it would be tucked away in a location where it wouldn't be noticed by the casual observer. It was while we were looking for the recording device that we found something else.

"Check this out," Cosmo said after moving a shelf with books that looked to be normal to the casual observer but was actually fake and easy to move aside. "A hidden wall safe."

Adam and I made our way to the back of the room where Cosmo stood. "Any idea how to open it?" I asked since safe cracking was not one of my specialties, and this one looked to be sturdy and secure.

Each member of the Geek Squad took turns taking a closer look at the safe, but none claimed to have any more of an idea how to open it than I did.

"If I know Bek, and I do," Skeet said, "the odds are that even if you could figure out the correct four-digit number sequence to open this door, there will be a second locked door behind it." He narrowed his gaze. "The guy is seriously paranoid. I don't think we should waste a lot of time on this."

"I guess seven combination locks to open one door is a bit paranoid," I said, glancing toward the front door, which likewise locked from the inside. "If Bek ever needs help. If he falls or has a heart attack or needs medical intervention of some sort, rescue personnel will never be able to get inside."

"I guess when you go to as much trouble to keep people out as Bek did, you have to consider the fact that you aren't just keeping the bad guys out; you're keeping everyone out," Chip said.

"You know," Ape said, "I wouldn't be at all surprised to find that Bek has a panic button."

"Panic button?" I asked.

"A way to remotely work the locks on the front door in the event he needed help but was injured and unable to unlock them himself."

I lifted a brow. "I guess that makes sense. He may even have the ability to control the locks with a device he wears on his body. Maybe a watch."

"A watch," Ape said. "Of course. Why didn't I think of that? Bek has a smartwatch that records all sorts of things. His heart rate, his movements, steps taken, caloric needs, and all sorts of other things he programmed it to do. If he was kidnapped and the kidnapper took his cell phone, maybe he didn't think to take his smartwatch."

"Can you access the data?" I asked.

"Yeah. I think I can," Ape said. He looked at Chip. "With Chip's help. We'll need a computer and an internet connection."

"Let's look around to see if we can find any surveillance tapes and then head back to my office," I suggested. "We can use the desktop computer. It's got more power than my laptop, and there's plenty of room for all of us to work." I took photos of a few of the whiteboards despite the fact that the kids felt that

Bek would be upset by that. I wasn't planning to steal his work. I just needed a record of some of the names he'd jotted down as he worked.

"I'll order pizza," Adam offered. He looked at me. "Rain check on the steak?"

I nodded as Chip began to examine the area near the monitor. Following a cable, he backtracked it to a hard drive that seemed to run the security system. It appeared to be a dedicated unit and would probably require a password to access. I wasn't sure I felt right about taking the hard drive since we still didn't know with any degree of certainty that the man was actually in trouble. After some discussion, we decided to start by seeing what we could learn by accessing the data stored by the smartwatch before removing anything from Bek's cabin. Skeet locked up, and the Geek Squad, Adam, and I headed back toward town.

Chapter 6

I called Jemma during our drive back toward town to ask her to let the dogs out. I told her about the smartwatch and our plan to try to access the data, and she suggested we all just come over to her place. She had a computer system that was much superior to the one in my office, plus, if there was anything she could do to help, she offered to try. Josie was home as well and offered to make a salad and dessert to go with the pizza. Adam called and ordered enough pizza for all of us, and the pizza place offered to deliver it to the cottage when it was ready, and then Adam and I, along with the Geek Squad, headed toward my office to pick up my vehicle and then to the peninsula for pizza and research.

Skeet immediately headed over to pet Kai and Kallie when we arrived at the roommates' cottage.

"I love dogs," Phoenix exclaimed. "Oh, and kittens," she screeched when she noticed Stefan and Damon barreling down the stairs when they heard us arrive.

"And check out that view," Cosmo said as he headed toward the sliding glass door leading out to the deck that overlooked the bay. "This would be the perfect place to set up a telescope."

Jemma had hauled out her laptop plus a second one for Chip to use, so the two computer nerds went to work trying to access Professor Beklund's smartwatch data while Skeet and Phoenix played with the animals, and Ape joined Cosmo on the deck. Adam sat down at the table with Jemma and Chip, so I joined Josie in the kitchen.

"So, how was Anne today?" I asked as Josie washed lettuce.

She paused. "She seemed skittish. In fact, she seemed downright terrified about something, but I couldn't get her to talk about it. She did her job and stayed for the whole shift, but when Parker came in to tell me about the man who'd been found shot to death, she looked like she was going to flee."

"Do you think whatever this woman is afraid of is tied to the dead man?"

Josie shrugged. "Maybe. I tried to ask Anne about it, but she wouldn't say a thing. When she left the bar and grill at the end of her shift, I had this odd feeling she wasn't coming back."

I slid onto a barstool. "You offered to help, and Anne decided not to accept. If she is running from someone, it's unlikely she'll trust anyone, which means there's little you can do unless she lets you in."

"Yeah. I guess. And I did try on more than one occasion to get Anne to tell me what was going on."

Josie went to the refrigerator and pulled out tomatoes and cucumbers.

"Is there anything I can do to help?" I asked.

"No. I'm just going to chop a few tomatoes to add to the salad, and I already made the dressing." She began dicing and chopping. "Actually," she amended, "if I know growing boys, and I think I do, we might want to set something out to snack on until the pizza arrives. I have three or four kinds of cheese in the cheese drawer and crackers in the cupboard over the refrigerator. Maybe you can make up a tray with some cheese, crackers, grapes, and apples."

I got up and began assembling the supplies I'd need.

"Do you know if the pizza place said how long it would be before the pizza arrives?" Josie asked.

"They said an hour," Adam answered. "I had them throw in a couple six-packs of soda as well."

I set the cheese tray on the table, along with a stack of paper plates and napkins. Cosmo and Ape must have noticed the food since they came in and joined their counterparts who'd already eaten half the cheese I'd sliced. I hoped Adam had ordered enough pizza. These kids were acting like they hadn't eaten in a week.

"In order to access the account that's synced up to the smartwatch, we'll need an email address, possibly a phone number, and a password," Jemma said after she'd spent a few minutes talking to Chip and surfing around on the internet. "Chip provided two email addresses, one personal and one professional, and I have his cell phone number from the records you all picked up yesterday. Does anyone have a guess as to a password?"

The five kids all offered guesses, but it was apparent that none of them knew what sort of password the man might have used. We tried his birthday, a couple mathematical terms Bek seemed to enjoy as well as the names of some of his favorite scientists and mathematicians. He didn't have a wife or kids, and as far as we knew, he didn't have a best friend whose name he might have used, so we tried famous number sequences as well as substitution ciphers. By the time the pizza arrived, we were no closer to accessing the account than we were when we started.

"Try Goldie," Phoenix suggested as she chowed down on her second slice of pepperoni pizza. "The guy doesn't have any family, but he told me the story of a pet fish named Goldie he had as a child."

"You know," Jemma said, getting up and crossing the room to the table where her laptop was still open and logged into, "that could work." She tried Goldie with both emails that had been offered. Neither worked. But then she entered Goldie with his cell phone number, and that led her to the account she was looking for.

Chip left his pizza on the table and got up to join her. "Is the smartwatch still transmitting data?" he asked.

"No. At least not the heart rate and that sort of thing. The GPS is still working, however."

"So, where is he?" Skeet asked.

She frowned. "Hang on." She typed in some commands. "It looks like he's at his cabin."

"At his cabin?" Cosmo asked.

"The smartwatch must be at the cabin," Ape said. "Maybe he took it off before whatever happened, happened."

"That would be my guess," Jemma said. "I'm not picking up movement or any sort of vitals, so I have to assume the smartwatch is idle."

I could see that the teens were disappointed that the smartwatch hadn't given us more information than it had. It must be frustrating to want to find someone so badly only to have it appear as if they had simply disappeared.

"It looks like there's a record of the data collected by the watch going back quite a while," Jemma said. "We might not be able to see where the professor is now, but we can see where he'd been before taking the smartwatch off and disappearing."

That seemed to get everyone's attention. "Where had Bek been just before disappearing?" Ape asked.

"According to the smartwatch's GPS history, it's been in the cabin or near the cabin for the past two weeks."

"Near the cabin?" Ape asked. "How near?"

"Within a quarter of a mile," Jemma answered. She pulled up a map on her computer screen and pointed to a location to the east of the cabin in a heavily wooded area. "What's right here?"

Ape leaned over her shoulder. "Nothing. There isn't anything east of the cabin other than forest and rocks and maybe a seasonal creek or two."

"I can't say for certain that Professor Beklund was the one wearing the smartwatch, but whoever was wearing it during the week before you found him missing had been going back and forth between the cabin and this location each day. Usually more than once a day."

Skeet walked over and peered over Jemma's shoulder as well. "We should check it out. See what's there."

I looked out at the now pitch-black sky. "It's too late to check it out now."

"I can do it in the morning," Skeet responded.

"I have a trig exam," Cosmo said. "I'd skip it, but I already have a makeup exam from when I was sick."

"Yeah," Chip agreed. "I should show at school as well. I'm trying to get into a really good college, and I need to watch my grades."

"Maybe we should wait and go after school," Ape suggested.

The kids all agreed to meet up after school the following day and see what they could find. Once that was settled, the teens confessed to having homework and needing to get home. I walked the kids out to their car, said my goodbyes, and then promised to speak to them the following afternoon. When I returned to the cottage, I began helping Josie clean up while Jemma talked to Adam about a new software program she was developing which she felt might be of use to him as he made the changes he'd planned to make within the foundation he ran. He seemed interested in what she had to share, but he had a long drive home, so he said his goodbyes and left after promising Jemma that they'd talk some more about her ideas. Just about the time Josie turned the dishwasher on, her cell phone rang. She looked at the caller ID. "It's Parker."

I watched her face as she listened to what Parker had to say. Her smile slipped into a frown after only a few seconds. She looked at me. "Anne's been arrested."

"Arrested?" I asked.

Josie nodded. She said a few things to Parker and then hung up.

"Arrested for what?" I asked after Josie set the cell phone down, and Jemma joined us in the kitchen.

"Murder. I guess the guy Parker found shot to death is Anne's ex-husband. Parker said the man's name was Braylon Dario, and Anne's real name is

Penelope Dario," Josie continued. "I guess Braylon was a rich attorney living in San Francisco when he met Penelope, a waitress at a downtown diner. He fell in love with her, the two married, and two years after they married, Penelope took off. Parker didn't know why, but she did say that Penelope has been running for almost a year."

"So Braylon caught up with her, and when Anne saw him at the bar and grill yesterday, she panicked and killed him," I said.

"That's what Deputy Todd thinks. Parker said that her contact in the public defender's office told her that Penelope insisted that she was innocent during her intake interview. Parker is going to see if she can find out more about what's going on."

"I wonder if we can get in to see her," I asked.

Josie shrugged. "I guess that depends on how agreeable Todd is this week. Parker said that Penelope is in the local jail awaiting arraignment, so if Todd is in a good mood, maybe one of us can get in to speak to her."

"I'm sure Parker will try, and she seems to know Todd the best, so I'm going to suggest we wait and talk to Parker in the morning before we do anything," Jemma suggested.

We all agreed that Jemma's plan to wait until we talked to Parker was a good one. I had to admit that I was more than just a little curious about the rest of the story, although I did have to admit that if the dead man was Anne's ex-husband, Todd had good reason to believe she was guilty.

"It does sound like this woman is guilty," Jemma voiced the exact same thought I'd just had.

"Anne wouldn't kill anyone," Josie defended.

"You just met this woman a few months ago," Jemma reminded her. "Sure, she seemed nice enough, but she also freaked when she saw the murder victim and took off to somewhere as of yet unidentified. The following day, she showed up at work as if nothing had happened. The only way she would feel confident to show up at the very place her ex-husband had looked for her the previous day would be if she knew he was dead and therefore no longer a threat."

"Yeah." Josie sighed. "I guess all of that is true. I wonder why she ran in the first place. I suppose the guy might have been abusive, but why not just divorce him. Why run?"

"Based on the yacht he arrived on, the guy looked to be really well off," I said. "I don't know for certain that the yacht belonged to him, of course. Parker thought it might not. But even if it didn't, the guy seemed to have been connected. Chances are he was an abuser who was too well connected to simply let his wife leave and embarrass him. Maybe she felt trapped with no way out, so she ran."

Josie didn't respond, but I could see the look of anger that crossed her face. I had the feeling there might be something behind that anger. Something more than just empathy or understanding. I'd known Josie for almost a year, but we'd never really discussed past relationships. Had she, perhaps, had her own experience with an abusive man who not only wanted to punish but dominate her as well? I decided not to ask. Not now. Maybe someday if the opportunity presented itself.

Chapter 7

Today, as the sun peeked its glorious head of gold over the horizon, I realized, was going to be a busy one. I knew Parker planned to head to the jail and try to talk to Anne, or more accurately, Penelope. I knew that if the woman was able to convince Parker that she was indeed innocent of the crime she'd been charged with, Josie would be depending on Jemma, Parker, and me to help her find the person who killed Penelope's ex-husband, thereby freeing the innocent woman. Jemma and I had both agreed to do whatever we could to help in that event. I knew, based on the small amount of information I already had, that proving such a thing might not be easy, but if Josie was convinced of the woman's innocence, we'd sure as heck try.

And then there was the case of the missing professor. I knew the Geek Squad was worried about the man, and while a part of me really did think he'd just taken off for some reason, I'd agreed to do what I could to help them figure things out, and I intended to try to do that as well. The kids had school today, so I figured I'd do what I could before their classes were over for the day. If I had news to share, I could call another meeting for later in the afternoon.

And finally, I hoped to work things out to get together with Adam. I didn't sense that he had anything urgent to talk to me about, but it would be nice to spend some time with the man. My search for answers relating to my past had stalled, and with that pause, the need for the two of us to meet and discuss what we'd discovered had diminished, which had unfortunately led to us spending less time together. Sometimes I wondered if we'd even be friends if not for the fact that his father had harbored me as a child, and as the son of the man who had most likely been privy to at least some of the answers I was after, he seemed to feel obligated to help me.

It was early still, so I decided to start my day with a run, which is the way I tried to start each day when I could. I rolled myself out of bed, headed into the bathroom, and then pulled on a pair of sweatpants, a sports bra, a stretchy tank, and an old worn hoodie. I dug out my filthy yet relatively new Nike's, called the dogs, and headed out the door.

I started off slowly to allow my muscles time to warm up. The sun rising in the east shone on the flat water of the bay while a cluster of dark clouds gathered to the west. I hadn't taken the time to check the weather report, but if the cloud bank in the west was any indication, I suspected that rain was in the forecast for later in the day. Of course, not all clouds led to rain. During the waning days of fall, the weather often proved to be unpredictable. It seemed that we'd had a pattern as of late of storms forming miles off the coastline, which, despite the afternoon breeze we often enjoyed, never quite made it onto the shore.

As I turned away from the bay to climb up to the bluff, I picked up the pace a bit. As the bluff trail leveled off, I slowed to enjoy the sound of the leaves crunching beneath my feet. I traveled the bluff trail almost every day, so I knew it well, but I still marveled at the beauty of packed dirt covered with leaves in shades of red, gold, and yellow.

When I reached the back fence of Adam's property, the dogs and I paused and then turned around and headed back to the cottage where I gave them food and fresh water and then headed toward the shower. I wasn't sure exactly what the day might bring, but I did suspect that I might be grateful to have chosen casual and comfortable clothing, so I settled on a pair of relatively new jeans, a silk blouse the color of new moss, and a cardigan in a dark shade of sable that almost exactly matched my knee-high boots. After drying my long blond hair, I pulled it back in a large barrette and then inserted small emerald studs into my ears.

Once I was dressed and ready to head out, I paused to consider whether or not to bring the dogs. I had a lot going on today, and it was more likely than not that I'd end up needing to leave them, so I decided it might be better to just leave them at the cottage in the long run. I called Jemma to let her know the dogs would be home and to ask her if she'd look in on them, which was when she informed me that Josie had spoken to Parker again and had news. She suggested I stop by before I headed out so she could catch me up. She also suggested that I just bring the dogs by and plan to leave them with her for the day. I agreed to both, grabbed my computer bag and backpack, and then headed next door.

"So, what's up?" I asked after Jemma invited me inside and offered me a cup of coffee. I noticed Josie wasn't home and figured she'd had an early shift and needed to go into work.

"Josie spoke to Parker, who had spoken to Deputy Todd. According to Todd, not only was Braylon Dario a very wealthy and highly respected attorney but according to Dario's law partner, the man had previously been attacked by Penelope after catching her with another man. The partner swore to Todd that it had been Braylon who'd kicked Penelope out rather than her running away."

"Really?" I said, a tone of doubt evident in my voice. "If he kicked her out and she wasn't on the run, why the name change? Why the job at the Rambling Rose? Even if Braylon and Penelope had a prenup of some sort, it's still likely she'd have come away from the marriage with something."

Jemma shrugged. "Parker asked Todd those very questions, and he simply said that according to

Dario's law partner, Penelope was an unstable woman with a fiery temper. It was the law partner's opinion that Braylon came to Gooseberry Bay to have Penelope sign papers relating to their divorce and that she went crazy and shot him."

I rolled my eyes. "That's totally nuts. The woman has obviously been hiding. If her rich and powerful husband really did kick her out and meant her no harm, why would she feel the need to hide?"

"Exactly." Jemma took a sip of her coffee. "Josie is really upset about the whole thing. Parker is too. We talked about getting together later to come up with some sort of strategy to help Penelope. Parker said that she'll be arraigned tomorrow, and it was Todd's opinion that the judge would not grant bail. If the story Todd seems to believe is true, she's run before and will run again."

I paused as I considered the situation. "You said that Todd told Parker that Penelope had been violent toward her husband in the past. Violent how? Exactly what is she supposed to have done?"

"According to Deputy Todd, during a previous argument, Penelope hit her husband over the head with a lamp hard enough to knock him out. It was this argument, along with her infidelity, that caused him to decide to divorce her."

"Did Braylon call the police at the time of the lamp incident?" I wondered.

"Parker said that Todd told her that, according to the law partner, Braylon hadn't called the police. It was his opinion that Braylon was embarrassed that the woman had gotten the better of him and decided to quietly divorce his wife rather than making a public spectacle of the crazy woman he'd had the misfortune of being seduced into marrying."

Wow, I thought to myself. That entire explanation sounded like a bunch of hooey. Not that I knew what had occurred and not that I knew Anne, or I guess Penelope, well enough to have an opinion as to the likelihood that she might become violent under the right circumstances, but the woman who I'd briefly met and the woman who Josie described didn't sound like a crazy or violent woman who was on the run from the law so much as a victim who was on the run from the man who abused her.

"What time are you meeting?" I asked.

"Josie gets off at four. Parker said she could be here no later than five. They both planned to try to speak to Penelope personally. I'm not sure if they'll be successful, but they both intend to try. If you want to come around when you're done in town for the day, we'll welcome your sleuthing know-how."

"I'm in," I said decisively. "I have some research to do relating to Professor Beklund, and I promised the Geek Squad that I'd be around to discuss things once they had a chance to look around the property where Beklund lives, but I can stop by after that."

"Great. We'll just get takeout. I'm sure Josie will be too riled up to cook."

"I'd offer to bring something, but I might get tied up, and I don't want everyone waiting for me."

"We'll just have something delivered once everyone gets here," Jemma suggested.

I stood up. "Okay, that's perfect. I'll call you later with an update. If the Geek Squad doesn't come up with any new information that would require an immediate follow-up, I should be here around four or four-thirty. If they do find something, and it looks like I'm going to be later than five, I'll let you know."

I chatted with Jemma for a few more minutes and then headed into town. The Beklund case was a tricky one since I really wasn't sure he was even in trouble. Still, I could see that the Geek Squad was worried about the man, and based on what I'd discovered to date, it did seem unlikely that the guy would just take off without telling anyone. Perhaps the man wasn't actually missing but had simply been avoiding everyone for some reason. I paused to think about that for a minute. A scenario where Beklund was actually hiding out on his property and avoiding the Geek Squad for one reason or another was a scenario that might be worth looking into. He had cameras positioned to announce a visitor well before that visitor would be close enough to view the cabin or any movement surrounding the cabin. It would be easy to simply slip out and hide until whoever had come visiting had left.

Once I arrived at my office, I pulled up the file I'd started on the case. At this point, the only lead I had was a list of four names that I'd found on the whiteboards in the cabin when we returned yesterday to look around: Armand Galveston, Nelson Atwater, Gordon Crabtree, and Balakin Antonov. Deciding to start with the first name, I punched it into my search engine. There were actually more people named Armand Galveston than I would have imagined, but I figured it would be easy to narrow things down. I finally settled on a man living in Pittsburgh, Pennsylvania. Professor Galveston taught at Carnegie Mellon University, specializing in the field of artificial intelligence. If, as the Geek Squad kids suspected, Professor Beklund had stumbled across a significant piece of information that might be of interest to those in the field, then it made sense that the man might have contacted those who specialized in such things.

I figured I'd call the Armand Galveston associated with the university in Pittsburgh and simply ask him if he knew Professor Beklund and if he'd spoken to him in recent days, but first, I wanted to look up the other names on the list to see if I could come up with some sort of pattern.

Like I had with Armand Galveston, I began with a general search using the name Nelson Atwater. There were fewer men with this name, and I was able to narrow things down fairly quickly to a man who was now retired but had been involved in research pertaining to artificial intelligence with Stanford University at one point. Closer, I realized, which made it more likely the men had known each other. Since Atwater was retired, I wouldn't be able to reach him through the university, so I'd need to deepen my search and hopefully come up with contact information.

It took me another two hours to nail down the information that Gordon Crabtree worked for Intelligene, and Balakin Antonov was a Russian citizen currently attending MIT on a student visa.

"Okay," I said aloud, even though I was the only one in my office. "I have a list with four names, all who were studying, working in, or have worked in the field of artificial intelligence, which is the same field Ronald Evington works in, who, according to Skeet, was after some sort of research Beklund was doing."

I paused and let the information I'd dug up ramble around in my mind a bit. Initially, my plan had been to identify all four men, contact them, and simply ask about Beklund. It seemed unlikely that any of the men on my list would know where the man was currently located. But they may have spoken to the professor and might be able to provide a clue of some sort that would help me understand where the man might have gone, if he had indeed, gone somewhere of his own free will. Additionally, all four men had likely heard of Ronald Evington since he was once a professor in the field and perhaps could offer a different viewpoint from that provided by Skeet and the others.

I leaned back in my chair, clicking my pen open and closed and debating where to start. The four men on the list were nothing more than names to me, so it seemed impossible to know who to begin with. Deciding to start with the first name on the list I'd made from those found on Beklund's whiteboards, I looked at the information I'd pulled up relating to Armand Galveston and dialed his office number at the university. I was surprised when he actually picked up.

"Professor Galveston, my name is Ainsley Holloway," I jumped right in. "I'm a private investigator who has been hired by a group to look into the disappearance of a man named Ivan Beklund."

"Bek is missing?"

"Perhaps," I answered with a tone of caution in my voice. No reason to get the man all riled up if Beklund was simply taking some time off, which, quite honestly, I still half expected. "I'm going to be honest with you and say right up front that I'm not certain that the man has met with foul play, but a group of high school students the professor seems to meet and work with on a regular basis came to me after the professor failed to show up at his cabin for more than a week. I went to look around with the group, and while everything appeared to be in order, there did seem to be reasons to suspect that things might not be as they should. I agreed to look into things, and one of the potential clues I came across was a list of four names penned on the whiteboards in his residence. I'm simply calling to ask if you've spoken to the man in recent weeks or have any idea where he may have gone off to."

"No," the man answered. "I haven't spoken to Bek in more than a year. Maybe two. We were never very close, but we did travel in the same academic circle at one point. The man is brilliant, but he's also somewhat unstable. When I first met him several decades ago, his mental health issues presented as quirks, but as he's aged, he's become increasingly paranoid. I guess you know that he quit his job and went into hiding a few years ago."

"Do you believe it's possible the man could have stumbled across some sort of information that might actually pose a threat to him?"

"It's doubtful," the man answered. "Bek is extremely gifted intellectually, but he has a hard time focusing and organizing his thoughts. He tends to hop around from one project to another, never really sticking with anything long enough to nail down a solution. I'm not saying it's impossible that he could have discovered something important. He certainly has the potential to do so, but having said that, it does seem sort of unlikely." He paused. "Do you happen to know what it is he supposedly came across that might have put him in danger of some sort?"

"Not specifically, but the group who hired me did mention the name Ronald Evington."

"Evington is an academic who went into the private sector decades ago. He works in artificial intelligence, which happens to be the field I specialize in, and we chat from time to time."

"Do you believe it's possible this man might prove to be a threat to Beklund?"

He chuckled. "No. Evington is at the top of his field, while Beklund only dabbles now that he's retired. I sincerely doubt there is anything Bek might know that Evington would be interested in."

"One of the teens specifically mentioned that Beklund has shared that he'd made a discovery that Evington would be interested in. He said that he needed to protect his equations from the man."

Galveston was silent for a moment. "Look, I really don't know what Bek might have stumbled across or if Evington would be interested in what he had, but I don't think Ronald is the sort of man who would kidnap or do harm to the professor just to access whatever information he might have floating around in his very disorganized mind. Evington might not have quite the IQ Beklund has, but he is much better at using his innate abilities. I sincerely doubt that Bek actually has anything worth stealing. Having said that, if I were you, I'd probably start by reaching out to Evington and asking him these questions. I assume you haven't done that."

"No," I admitted. "Not yet. I guess I just wanted to get a better feel for the situation before I actually called the man."

"Ronald is a good guy. Not only is he a very competent scientist, but he's an excellent businessman who has done very well financially. I really don't think he'd have any reason to do harm to a kook like Bek. Call him. I think he may be able to clear all of this up."

I thanked the man and wished him well, and then I hung up. I paused to go over the conversation in my mind. The guy hadn't said a thing to cast suspicion on either Evington or himself, yet I had picked up a vibe that wasn't evident in the words he spoke so much as in the tone. If there was something going on and

Galveston was privy to it, then chances were the man was already on the phone to Evington. If my imagination had gotten the better of me and the subtext I'd picked up was all in my mind, then waiting to call Evington until I had more still seemed to be the best bet. I pondered my next move, eventually deciding to call Nelson Atwater. Atwater had worked in research pertaining to artificial intelligence with Stanford University but had since then retired. I'd need to find contact information for the man, but he still seemed my best bet. Gordon Crabtree worked for Intelligene, Ronald Evington's company, so if something was going on, chances were Crabtree was in on it. Balakin Antonov was still a student, so it was less likely he'd know the details of Bek's work. Still, Bek did seem to enjoy teens and young adults, whereas he didn't seem to have a lot of use for most adults. Maybe Antonov would know something. I looked up his number, called, and left a message asking him to call me.

I thought about what I knew and what I most wanted to know, which brought me to the cabin and the land that came with the cabin. One of the Geek Squad members had mentioned that Professor Beklund had moved to the area three years ago. That wasn't all that long ago, so it seemed reasonable that I might be able to dig up information about the purchase of the property. Turning back toward my computer, I pulled up records relating to transfers of titles. It didn't take long to find that someone named Beth Willis had sold the land where the cabin now sat to Beklund five years ago. I supposed that made sense. While he didn't move to the area until three years ago, it did make sense that the man had planned his escape from academic life before making his move, and, given the specifics of the cabin, it also made sense that it was custom built to meet Beklund's needs. I wasn't sure that a conversation with Beth Willis would provide me with any information I didn't already have, but I decided to give the woman a call and see what she knew.

Unfortunately, the call went to voicemail. I left my name, phone number, and the reason for my call, and then I turned back to my notes. I was about to call the next name on my list when Parker blew in through the front door.

"Any news about Penelope?" I asked as Parker sat down across from me.

She nodded. "All bad. I spoke to Deputy Todd, and he seems to be completely convinced that Anne, or I guess I should say Penelope, is a nutcase who unsuccessfully tried to kill her husband in the past and managed to finish the job two days ago. The arraignment is tomorrow, and Todd seems confident that the judge will deny bail. That means Penelope will have to sit in jail until her trial."

"Does she have an attorney?" I asked.

Parker shrugged, "I'm sure one has been assigned to her, although I'm not sure who that might be." She blew out a breath. "I don't suppose it matters. There isn't an attorney working for the public defender's office who will stand much of a chance once Dario's partner gets involved."

I paused to think about the situation. I wanted to believe that Penelope was innocent since Josie really seemed to care about her, but all I could think about was how Penelope had fled the bar and grill when her ex-husband had come in but then had shown up for work the next day as if nothing had happened. Penelope must have known that the man was dead and therefore no longer a threat even though the body had yet to be found when she'd arrived at work the next day. Of course, if Penelope had killed him, why didn't she run? Why even return to the Rambling Rose, where she knew the police would easily be able to catch up with her?

"How certain are you that Penelope actually is innocent?" I asked.

Parker frowned. "Honestly, I'm not all that confident. Fifty-fifty at best. Josie seems certain that the woman she's been working with for the past few months isn't a killer, and while I don't know the woman well, I have spoken to her from time to time, and I didn't pick up the killer vibe, but I guess it's hard to say what someone might do if they feel threatened." Parker paused briefly before continuing. "The thing is that while I might not have any data to support her innocence, my gut is telling me that this woman didn't kill her ex-husband. As we've discussed, it makes no sense that she would run away from her very affluent life, change her name, and take a job as a waitress in a small, out of the way place like Gooseberry Bay if she didn't feel that her life was in danger."

"Okay," I said, "That's good enough for me. I know we're planning to meet at Jemma and Josie's this evening. Is there anything I can do to help you in the meantime?"

"Actually," Parker said, glancing at her watch. "I need to go. I was passing by, saw you sitting here, and decided to come in and vent a little, but I have a meeting with the mayor relating to another matter and shouldn't be late. I'll see you this evening. Maybe if we all put our heads together, we can figure this out."

"Okay. Thanks for the update, and I'll see you later."

After Parker left, I decided to do a bit of digging on my own. I was sure Jemma would have come up with whatever I found by the time we met, but I was curious and wanted to have an overview before our get-together this evening. I began by typing the name Penelope Dario into my search engine. I already knew that Penelope, a waitress working in a downtown diner, had met and married Braylon Dario, a wealthy businessman living in San Francisco. The couple had been married for two years when Penelope disappeared. According to what we suspected, Penelope had been running for over a year. She'd been in Gooseberry Bay working for the Rambling Rose using the name Anne Jorgenson for a few months. I didn't know where she'd been before that or why she'd run in the first place.

I decided to look at Penelope's history before marrying Dario as a starting place. A quick search of public records told me that Penelope Cotter married Braylon Dario in June of two thousand eighteen.

Using that information, I was able to pull up multiple news articles of the event itself. I paused to consider the photo of a smiling bride and groom standing on a balcony overlooking the sea. I wasn't sure where the photo had been taken. I assumed somewhere close to San Francisco since both the bride and groom called the area home. It was a bright sunny day with only the ocean in the backdrop.

Penelope looked different in her wedding photo. As Anne, she sported short black hair and brown eyes, I assumed that she was wearing colored contacts, but in her wedding day photo, she had long blond hair, pulled up in the front and on the sides and then allowed to trail down her slender tanned back, and her bright blue eyes shone with happiness as she looked into the eyes of the man, who I assume, at that moment, she considered to be her prince charming.

She wore a simple strapless gown that hugged her slender body, but the tiara that held the veil in place was studded with sapphires and diamonds that must be worth a fortune.

As she gazed into the eyes of her new husband, she rested one hand on his chest. I couldn't be sure if the pose had been staged to show off the huge diamond ring she wore on her left hand or if the placement of her hand over his heart had been a genuine gesture of affection. Either way, the look of adoration in her eyes seemed to be genuine. What had happened to cause this woman to run, I wondered. She looked to be so in love. I supposed Penelope wouldn't be the first woman to marry her prince charming, only to realize he was an ogre in disguise once the honeymoon was over.

Digging further, I was able to determine that Penelope Cotter had been born on September seventh, nineteen ninety-three, which made her twenty-eight. My research had revealed the fact that Braylon Dario was forty-seven, which made Penelope nineteen years his junior. Penelope must have been twenty-four or twenty-five when the couple first met. I wasn't sure how long the pair had dated before marrying, but either way, Penelope would most likely have been young and impressionable when her prince charming swept into the diner where she waited tables and swept her off her feet.

Penelope had grown up in a small town in Northern California, where she graduated high school when she was seventeen. I wasn't sure if Penelope left for San Francisco immediately or if she stayed around for a while, but I couldn't find any record of her going to college. I supposed I wouldn't be surprised to find that the beautiful young woman had fled the small town for the high energy of the larger city shortly after she turned eighteen. If I continued to search, I could most likely find her work history before taking the job at the diner where she met Braylon, but I didn't figure that information was all that important at this point, so I moved on.

Penelope was an only child who'd been raised by her mother. The father, whose name was listed on her birth certificate as Jeffery Baldwin, didn't appear to have been a part of her life. I made a note to look into that situation in more depth once I'd completed my overview. It appeared that while Penelope was both beautiful and popular, with roles of both head cheerleader and homecoming queen, she wasn't all that good a student and barely managed to graduate with the minimum required GPA. As I continued to dig around, I found a news article from the local newspaper published in the town where she grew up announcing that Penelope had been cast in a reoccurring role in a popular sitcom and was headed to LA. The article was written in two thousand twelve. I wondered if she'd ever gone off in search of her dream or if something had occurred before that landing her in San Francisco.

Again, I made a note to look into things in more depth, but the reality was that what occurred before Penelope began working at the diner and meeting Braylon was probably less important than what came after.

I decided to take a quick look at Braylon and his life before meeting Penelope and then refocus on the couple after the wedding.

Braylon Dario was born to and raised by a wealthy couple living in San Francisco. It appeared that Braylon attended the best schools, private through high school. He had two advanced degrees, including a law degree. Upon graduation, he worked for his father's law firm before jumping to a rival firm where he'd quickly made partner. The guy had been smart, no doubt about it. Not only had he gone to the best colleges, but he'd excelled. I was curious whether or not the man had been married before meeting and marrying Penelope, but all I could find was mention of an engagement when he was still in law school that didn't seem to have resulted in an actual wedding. I made a note to look into that further as well.

Okay, I thought to myself, so this rich, intelligent, successful, and probably entitled man in his mid-forties wanders into a downtown diner and spots a beautiful waitress in her mid-twenties. She has an enchanting smile, innocent eyes, and a gentle way about her that causes this successful attorney to take a second look. He strikes up a conversation with her, and at some point, he convinces her to go out with him. After a whirlwind affair, they marry, and then what? As I focused on the photo of the happy couple on their wedding day, I wondered how this couple got from there to here. I thought about the shy woman I'd met at the bar and grill a few times and supposed the easiest way to get that answer was just to ask Penelope if, in fact, one of us could get in to speak to her.

Chapter 8

I'd decided to do a search for previous warrants for both Braylon and Penelope when my cell phone rang. It was my cousin, money manager, and good friend, Warren Cornwall.

"Hey, Warren," I greeted the man who, until I'd learned the truth about what really went down when I was a child, I'd considered as being public enemy number one. "I'm glad you called. It's been a few weeks, and I've been thinking we needed to catch up."

"The family and I decided to spend some time at the villa on the coast, but we're home now, so I wanted to check in with you. How's everything been?"

"Good. Really good," I answered. "Busy. How's Giovanna and the kids?"

"The family is good. Everyone says hi. Giovanna is hoping you might consider coming to Italy for Christmas. We really do it up big," he persuaded. "Big trees in every room. Parties, balls, charity events, and gifts for the children's hospital. The ballet, the opera, and carriage rides under the stars. The Cornwall family is known for putting the merry in Christmas."

It sounded magical, but I thought about last Christmas here in Gooseberry Bay. It had been one of the most perfect holidays of my life with Adam, Jemma, Josie, and the rest of the peninsula gang. They were my family now, and during the holidays, when memories of Christmases with the my dad often made me a little sad, I needed to be with my family. "You know, I'd love to visit, but I've already promised to help out with the Christmas festival here in town. Maybe I can come after. Maybe even for New Year's Eve and New Year's Day."

"That would be wonderful. You know that you are always welcome any time it works out for you to make the trip."

"I know, and that means a lot to me. I imagine that Christmas in Italy would be magical. Maybe I'll plan to make the trip at some point."

"If you do, plan on coming early, so you can attend the Christmas Markets. I promise the experience is like nothing you've ever experienced."

"I've seen photos. It looks lovely." I had to agree.

Warren and I took the next thirty minutes to catch up before he finally got around to the real purpose of his call. "So I heard from the private investigator I hired to look into things on my end." I knew that, and while I was, in fact, a private investigator with the know-how to conduct my own investigation, Warren felt, and I agreed, that finding Avery, my missing sister, was important enough to have several people approaching the mystery of her disappearance from different angles. "It turns out that during her time in Italy, Marilee met a woman named Willamina Krause, and, based on what the man I have working on this was able to uncover, the two became friends."

"So you think Willamina might be Wilma?" It had never before occurred to me that Wilma might not be an American. I knew very little about the woman other than the fact that she'd helped Marilee run with Avery and me, but I guess I always assumed that Marilee had known Wilma from her life in the States before heading to Italy.

"I think it is a possibility," Warren said. "I don't know anything for certain at this point, but I think it is an avenue worth exploring."

"Yes," I said. "I agree that the idea that Marilee met Wilma while in Italy is worth a second look. At this point, figuring out who Wilma is and finding her seems to be our best bet at finding Avery." I paused to consider this. "I wonder if it was Wilma who gave Marilee the idea to take Avery and me to the States and then run with the money."

"Perhaps," Warren said. "It's too early to know for certain, but the man I hired did conduct a background check on Willamina Krause, and it does appear that she is, or was, the sort of person to be involved in what really boils down to kidnapping and embezzlement."

I closed my eyes as I tried to remember the woman. Dark hair cut short, young, probably early to mid-twenties. She hadn't been around all that long when Marilee left Piney Point with me, so my image of her was vague and blurry. I didn't remember the woman as being particularly nice or mean, but I did remember being afraid of both Marilee and Wilma. Of course, that might simply have been because I'd recently lost my parents and been torn from my home, which would have made it hard for me to trust anyone. "Okay, I'm listening," I said. "What did you find out?"

Warren cleared his throat and then began. "Willamina was born in Southern Germany to a large family with few financial resources."

"So she was born into poverty."

"She was," he confirmed. "The oldest of eight children, she took to the streets when she was still a teenager. As could be predicted, she fell in with a bad crowd and ended up dropping out of school before completion. Willamina's life after taking to the streets is a bit sketchy at this point. She doesn't appear to have been gainfully employed, and we've been unable to find any reference to a residence. She likely lived on the street and probably stole or begged for what she had. At some point, Willamina moved to Italy, where she got a job as a bartender in a back alley club. It appears that it was while working at this club that she met Marilee."

I knew that Marilee went to Italy to care for Avery and me after our parents were killed in a small plane crash. I also knew Marilee eventually convinced Warren it was best for everyone if she brought the one and three-year-old children to the States where she would have help from family members. I wasn't sure how long Marilee had been in Italy before deciding to return to the States. "So, how long was Marilee in Italy?" I asked.

"Three months. Marilee hired a woman named Ginny Gray to help take care of you and Avery, so she had a certain amount of freedom to do her own thing. Apparently, what I didn't know at the time but have since learned, is that what she most enjoyed doing was clubbing."

"Okay," I exhaled. "So at some point during the three months Marilee lived in Italy, she met Willamina, and the two became friends."

"Yes," Warren confirmed. "I'm not sure how long it was after Marilee met Willamina that Marilee decided to take you and Avery to the States, but it couldn't have been all that long. We suspect at this point that Marilee's plan had been to make off with your inheritance all along. We know that Marilee took you to the house on Piney Point and left you with Kingston Winchester, who hired the woman you referred to as Winnie to take care of you and Avery. And we know that I continued to put ten thousand dollars a month into an account for you and ten thousand dollars a month into an account for Avery until you turned nineteen. Someone, probably Marilee, withdrew the cash each month, and at this point, I can only assume that was her intent all along." He paused and then continued. "Actually, her initial plan may have been even grander since, in the beginning, she asked that I turn over the management of your inheritance to her. I declined to do so and offered the monthly support payment instead."

"Yes. I remember some of this. I remember that Marilee dropped us off with Kingston, and while she did come back from time to time, I guess to keep up appearances and check on us, she didn't stay at the estate. And I remember that eventually, Wilma showed up. Based on what Adam and I have been able to figure out, Marilee told Kingston that she planned to move the children, and Wilma was there to help with the trip. Also, based on what we've figured out, it appears that Marilee took me and headed to Georgia, where she left me with her friend, Daria Glen, and Wilma took Avery to a location we've yet to identify. I don't suppose the PI you hired has figured this part out as well."

"No," Warren confirmed. "At this point, he only suspects that Wilma and Willamina are the same person. I emailed you a packet that includes a photo of Willamina that was taken before she left Germany. I know there are residents currently living in Gooseberry Bay who lived in the area in nineteen ninety-five, and someone might remember seeing Wilma during her brief stay at the house on Piney Point. I hoped you could track one of these long-term residents down and confirm whether or not the two are the same woman."

"I can do that. In fact, I'll do it today if I can catch someone at home. Tomorrow at the latest."

"Tomorrow is fine. It's late here, and I plan to turn in after we conclude our conversation. Once you have confirmation that Willamina and Wilma are, in fact, the same person, we'll dig into Willamina and see what we can find."

I blew out a breath. "Okay. That sounds good. Maybe if we can finally figure out who Wilma was, we'll be able to track her down. Fingerprints and that sort of thing."

"That's the plan at this point."

I paused, almost afraid to ask my next question. "Do you think Wilma knows what happened to Avery? Do you think if we find Wilma, we'll find my sister as well?"

Warren blew out a long slow breath. "I don't know. I hope so. I suspect that Wilma may have handed Avery off the way Marilee handed you off to Daria, but I guess there's no way to know that with any degree of certainty until we catch up with her."

"We have to find her."

"We will. One way or the other, we will."

I glanced out the window of my office toward the dark blue bay. The boardwalk was almost deserted today, and many of the little carts and booths were closed until the weekend. I loved the hustle and bustle of a busy summer day, but during the off-season, when the pace of life slowed and the town was mostly free of tourists, I appreciated the quiet as well.

"Do you know anything more about Willamina? Is she still in touch with her family? Might they know how to find her?"

"My investigator spoke to a brother who shared that Willamina simply disappeared after leaving Germany. No one in the family has seen or heard from her in over twenty-five years. Most assume that she's dead. The brother shared that she was the wild sort. She was never content and was always looking for a way to glide through life with minimal effort on her part. The brother had no idea if his older sister had actually been part of a plan to kidnap two children in order to steal their inheritance, but he did say that he wouldn't be a bit surprised if she had been involved."

My heart sank. It appeared as if Marilee had been part of the plan to steal my inheritance, but she had left me with someone she trusted. She could have just killed me and dumped my body in the sea, but she hadn't, so she must have cared on some level. I just hoped that Wilma took the time to make sure Avery was safe before she disappeared. Not knowing was really the worst sort of feeling imaginable.

Deciding to call Adam to fill him in and ask his advice on selecting the best person to confirm or deny that Willamina was Wilma, I pulled my cell phone out and punched in his number.

"Ainsley. How are you this morning?" Adam greeted after answering.

"I'm great. Thanks for asking. Listen, the reason I'm calling is to fill you in on a conversation I had with Warren. Do you have a few minutes?"

"I do. What did Warren have to say?"

I took the next fifteen minutes to fill Adam in and to ask his advice. He suggested that we start by calling Winnie, the woman who'd been contracted to take care of Avery and me that summer. Since Adam knew Winnie well, he offered to send her the photo if I could email it to him. I assured him I was able to do so and would right then. He promised to call and speak to Winnie right away and then call me back after he'd spoken to her. I was anxious to find out as much as I could now that it looked like we'd picked up a new lead, but I knew that the first step was simply to confirm that Willamina and Wilma were indeed the same person.

Deciding to go back to my search for previous warrants for both Braylon and Penelope while I waited to hear from Adam, I started with Braylon and found a rap sheet that was both extensive and varied. "Interesting," I said aloud as I scanned through the long list of arrests for assault, domestic abuse, destruction of property, reckless driving, and multiple drug and alcohol-related offenses. Most everything I found had taken place when the man was in his teens and twenties, but there seemed to be little doubt that the guy liked to hit the bottle. When he did, he got mean. The really sad part about the whole thing was that it looked as if he never suffered anything more than a slap on the wrist despite what anyone could see was a pattern. I guess having a lot of money really did make the difference between doing time and being slapped with a fine or community service.

As I scanned the files I'd managed to pull up, it seemed clear to me that Penelope had been a battered wife, as we suspected. Unfortunately, despite the numerous 911 calls made by neighbors, the police never could get Penelope to press charges. I'd worked with women in similar situations who could never be convinced to leave the men who'd hurt them. Based on the fact that Penelope was now living in Gooseberry Bay as Anne, something must have occurred that effectively proved to be the last straw.

I frowned as I continued to read the reports submitted by police officers who'd been called out to the house by neighbors only to be sent away when Penelope provided an explanation for her bloody lip or black eye that didn't include her husband hitting her. So many. Too many to actually have been anything other than what it clearly was.

Leaning back in my chair, I rested my arms on the armrests of my chair and closed my eyes. I needed a minute to let the anger curling in my belly dissipate a bit so I could think clearly. Penelope had come to Gooseberry Bay using an assumed name. Whatever explanation she was willing to give or not give, it seemed apparent that she was on the run from someone. I supposed it was possible the person or situation she was running from was someone or something other than her ex-husband, but the fact that she took off in the middle of a shift when he showed up at the bar and grill where she worked indicated otherwise.

And then there was the fact that the man was dead. Shot in the back. According to Josie, Penelope was acting like nothing was going on. The fact that she'd shown up at work before the body of her ex-husband had been found seemed to indicate to me that she knew it was safe to go on with her life because the man was no longer a threat to her. The most obvious reason she'd know he was dead before anyone else did was because she killed him. Deputy Todd realized that as well, which is why he'd arrested her. I hated to agree with the man, but in this case, it did seem that his theory really was the obvious explanation.

Of course, Josie believed in Penelope and her assertion of innocence, and as long as Josie believed, I guessed I'd suspend my disbelief.

If Penelope really was innocent of killing the man, she was going to have an uphill battle convincing anyone else of that. Perhaps she knew what really happened and could provide information that would allow Deputy Todd to track the actual killer down. I supposed in that situation, she might get off without having to spend a whole lot of time in jail while everyone sorted things out. Josie planned to try to speak to Penelope today. At this point, I guessed all I could do was wait to see what she found out.

I jotted down a few notes and had resorted to doodling when Adam called back to let me know that Winnie had confirmed that the woman she met twenty-five years ago who'd been using the name Wilma was indeed the same woman Warren's PI had identified as German-born Willamina. I called Warren and left him a voicemail. For the first time in a long time, I felt we actually had a viable lead to follow up on.

Chapter 9

I knew the Geek Squad planned to head out to Beklund's cabin to have a look around the grounds after school let out for the day. According to his smartwatch, the man had visited a specific GPS location on his land a number of times during the week before he disappeared, and the gang wanted to find out why. They planned to head over to my office when they were done so we could discuss what they might have found. I planned to meet up with Jemma, Josie, and Parker to work on Penelope's case that evening, but I figured I could meet with the kids at four and still make it to the roommates' cottage by five. I still hadn't found contact information for Nelson Atwater, who appeared to have left the country after retiring, so I decided to work on that while I waited. Given the fact that Beklund had Atwater's name on one of the whiteboards, it seemed as if he may have planned to contact him and might have the contact information in his possession. Of course, it was possible that Atwater's name was on the whiteboard as a reminder for Bek to compare his findings to work Atwater had done in the past or review one of his publications in which a similar topic may have been explored.

I tapped the end of my pen on the desk in front of me. The reality was that without a pattern or some sort of context, I really had no idea why Beklund had listed the names of the four men. Armand Galveston had indicated that he hadn't spoken to Beklund in years. Either he was lying, and I didn't know why he would be, or Beklund had never planned to contact him, or, if he had planned to do so, he hadn't gotten around to doing so.

I was about to give up on the whole thing, at least for today, when I received a call back from Balakin Antonov.

"Mr. Antonov," I said after answering. "Thank you so much for calling me back."

"You said you were inquiring about Ivan Beklund," he responded with a heavy Russian accent.

"Yes. It seems Beklund may be missing. I can't say with any certainty if he left the area of his own free will or if foul play was involved, but I've been hired by some friends of his to track him down. I found your name among his list of contacts." I'd decided to take a slightly different approach than I had with Galveston.

"Yes, I know Professor Beklund. Nice guy. A little odd but nice nonetheless."

"Have you seen or spoken to him recently?"

"How recently?"

"Within the past couple of months?"

"No," he answered. "Bek and I spoke on the phone maybe six months ago. He was working on one of his equations, and he wanted to run some ideas past me. I listened to what he had and gave my advice."

"Did it seem like he was onto something?" I wondered.

"Not really." He took a deep breath. "Look, I like the guy. I met him when I was still in high school, and he helped me pull together some ideas I had but couldn't quite organize. I'm certain it was his guidance that helped me get into MIT. I owe the guy, and we have stayed in touch, but I won't say we're really all that close. We talk on the phone from time to time, but to be honest, I've begun to avoid his calls."

"Oh? And why is that?"

He hesitated. I didn't think he was going to answer, but eventually, he did. "Like I said, I like the guy, and I really do owe him, but the past few years, his mental health has begun to decline. I feel like he's somewhat out of touch with reality. The last conversation we had really just consisted of him rambling on and on about cracking the code and needing to keep what he'd found safe."

"Safe from whom?" I asked.

"He didn't say exactly. I think he was trying to protect humanity as a whole. He really wasn't making much sense. Some of what he said seemed to be based on actual science, but most of it was pure nonsense."

I hated to say it, but it looked like a pattern was beginning to emerge. If Beklund actually had lost his marbles, was it possible he really was simply hiding out somewhere? I thanked the man for getting back to me and asked him to call me if he heard from Beklund. My initial impression was that the man had simply taken off, and the more I learned, the more convinced I was that my initial impression would most likely prove to be correct.

The question was, where had the man gone if he had indeed taken off of his own free will? His car was still parked in the lot, and his cabin was a long way from town. Too far to comfortably walk. I supposed he might have hired a car. That was an idea to look into, and I was actually reaching for my list of car ride companies when my cell phone rang. It was Beth Willis calling me back. I hadn't really thought that a conversation with the woman would provide a new clue to follow, so I was pleasantly surprised when the information exchanged provided me with what I hoped was just the thing I needed to solve the case.

"I think it's cool that Bek has a bomb shelter," Chip said after I'd called the Geek Squad and told them to come by my office before heading out to

Beklund's place to look around. "I've always thought it would be awesome to have a place to go if the zombie apocalypse ever becomes a reality."

"I agree that it would be awesome to have a bunker to hide out in, but why does Bek have a bunker?" Phoenix asked as the six of us were all in my SUV heading toward Bek's property.

"The real estate agent I spoke to told me that the property had been owned by a man named Owen Wexler who built the bunker back in the sixties. According to the woman I spoke to, the bunker is camouflaged so that no one other than those given access would even know it was there. She also said that other than the bunker, the land was undeveloped when Bek purchased the property. I would imagine that when Professor Beklund purchased the property, he built the cabin well away from the bunker so he wouldn't draw attention to it. If not for the fact that this woman knew of the existence of the bunker, we'd never have found it."

"So the GPS location that Bek kept walking to and from in the days before he disappeared is probably where the bunker is located," Skeet said.

"I think so," I confirmed. "I marked the spot on my map program, and the real estate agent described the setting where we'll find the trap door which leads to a stairway leading into the bunker below."

"So maybe Bek did take his work and is hiding out there," Ape said.

"That makes sense to me," I agreed.

"But why wouldn't he tell us what he was doing?" Skeet asked. "We're his friends. He knows he can trust us."

"I think," I carefully began, "that Bek may have had a mental breakdown of some sort. I spoke to two of the four men whose names I found on the whiteboards, and both seemed to think he'd lost his grip on reality."

"Maybe they just aren't smart enough to understand what the man was working on," Skeet said defensively.

"Perhaps," I agreed. "But given what we know, it does seem likely that Bek never left his property. His car is in the lot. There was no sign of a struggle. We know he was concerned about his work. And we know he has a bunker where he can be fairly certain that no one will find him. Maybe he hasn't even spent all his time there. Maybe he just stashed the work he was concerned about there, and then when his perimeter alarm is sounded, he heads there."

I could see that both Skeet and Ape were resistant to that explanation, but the other three seemed to be open to the idea that the man simply had gone off the deep end and was hiding from threats that existed only in his mind.

When we arrived at the property, Skeet and Ape hurried ahead. I decided to let them. I was sure they'd try the cabin first and then head toward the location of the bunker as marked on the map. Of course, even if they were able to find the door to the bunker, there was no guarantee that Bek would open it, given the fact that he'd apparently hidden it from them in the first place. Of course, until we actually made contact with the man, the theory that the guy was simply hiding out and wasn't actually in danger was really only a theory.

By the time Phoenix, Chip, Cosmo, and I reached the cabin, Skeet and Ape were already standing in front of the structure.

"The cabin is still empty," Skeet said. "Everything looks the same."

"Let's take a look," I suggested.

Skeet opened the door, and everyone went inside. As Skeet had said, everything did look the same as it had the last time we were here. Unless Bek had been very careful to make things appear undisturbed, it really did look as if the man hadn't returned to the cabin since we'd been here Monday.

"Let's see if we can find the bunker," I suggested. "I don't know for certain that Bek's been hiding out there, but at this moment, it's really the only option I can think of."

Skeet locked the cabin up, and we headed toward the location where the bunker was supposed to be located. It really was very well hidden, and it took the six of us twenty minutes to find the door. Of course, finding the door didn't grant us access. Skeet tried the door, but like the door on the cabin, someone had added a multi-lock security system that one would need a series of codes to access.

"So what now?" Cosmo asked.

"I guess we just assume the guy is inside and let him be," Chip said. "What more can we do?"

Ape looked like he might cry. Phoenix put an arm around him.

"You have the man's cell phone number as well as his email," I pointed out. "Why don't you just leave him a message and let him know you're worried about him. Ask him to respond to the call or email. Maybe he will."

The group agreed that might be the best play at this point. I felt bad for the kids, but I certainly didn't know how to break into his fancy security system. Even if I was able to break in, for all I knew, once the door opened, it was possible that the individual breaking in would be met with a shotgun.

Chip and Cosmo headed back toward the cabin. Skeet hesitated but eventually followed. Ape looked like he was going to argue, but Phoenix took his hand, and he went along peacefully enough, but I could see that this was far from over. When we arrived at the cabin, Ape paused and looked down. He kicked the dirt with his tennis shoe.

"There's something here," he said.

"Oh? What?" I asked.

He bent down and brushed the top layer of dirt away. "It looks like blood."

I walked over and joined him. It did look like there was blood on the ground, although it also appeared that someone had gone to a lot of trouble to cover it up. I took my cell phone out and took a photo. "I'll need to call Deputy Todd."

"It's probably just deer blood," Skeet said. "I know he's not supposed to, but Bek hunts sometimes."

"It might be deer blood," I said. "But we need to be sure."

I could see the kids weren't happy about my calling in the cops, but if the red spots in the dirt were blood, calling Todd was the right thing to do. While I made my call, Skeet went inside the cabin. When he returned, he had the hard drive we'd found the previous day. I wasn't sure taking it was the best idea, but I knew Deputy Todd well enough to have zero faith in his ability to figure out what was really going on. If we were able to access the hard drive and there was surveillance footage to watch, that might give us the information we'd need to actually solve the case.

Todd arrived, took a sample of the dirt, and then left. Once Deputy Todd left, the teens and I left as well. The ride back to my office where Skeet had left his car was a mostly silent one. Chip offered to work on the hard drive, but I figured Jemma was more likely to have success accessing it, so I suggested that I take it to her. Skeet argued on Chip's behalf, but eventually, the Geek Squad as a whole agreed to let Jemma take a stab at it. In return, I agreed to call them the minute we got in. That was if we were, in fact, able to get in.

As the kids piled out of my SUV, I reminded them about the haunted house the following day.

They all promised to show up. I'd hoped we'd have this case solved by this point, so the kids could relax and enjoy the festival without worrying about their friend. Maybe Beklund would answer the emails the kids intended to send him. If the man was having a mental breakdown of some sort, he might need medical attention. If he was simply lost in his own fantasy, I still hoped he'd touch base with his friends, so they could set aside their worries and get on with their lives.

Chapter 10

When I arrived at the roommates' cottage, we all agreed to have dinner first, and then we'd discuss the case. Josie had made a thick and creamy shrimp chowder, which she served with hot bread and a huge green salad. A bottle of wine was opened and consumed, and despite the serious nature of the talk we all knew we'd have to have at some point, for that one hour, we were just a group of gal pals having a meal together.

We chatted about the upcoming Halloween Festival as well as the festive atmosphere of the boardwalk area now that all the decorations had been set into place. We talked about hosting a dinner party the following week, inviting Tegan, Booker, Coop, and Hope, as well as Adam and Archie if they were in town. We made plans to get together for our own holiday festivities once the events in town had come to an end, and we talked about the feasibility of heading to the pumpkin patch next week to buy gourds to carve and display outside our individual cottages.

Once the food had been consumed and the dishes cleared, we all settled in to hear what Parker had to say.

"As you know, I managed to talk Deputy Todd into allowing me to speak to Penelope, off the record, of course. He stayed within earshot, I suppose to ensure that I didn't abuse the privilege he was affording me, so I'm not sure Penelope felt comfortable telling me everything she knows, but I do feel like I got enough to get the gist of what probably happened." Parker took a sip of her coffee and continued. "Anyway, as we've already dug up, Penelope grew up in a small town in Northern California, where she enjoyed popularity but never really did well academically. She left home as soon as she graduated and made her way down to LA. Her acting career never really panned out. Eventually, Penelope landed in San Francisco, where she worked as a waitress in the downtown diner where she met her husband, a wealthy and successful attorney. She shared that she was immediately smitten with him, with his soft smile, gorgeous eyes, and sophisticated air, so when he asked her out, she jumped at the chance. She admitted that he was almost two decades older than her twenty-four years when they met, but she'd been unsettled and was looking for a foundation, so someone like him was exactly the sort of man she felt she needed. Their courtship was brief. They fell in love, got engaged, and then married in just a little over a year. She said that in the beginning, he was so very sweet and she was so very happy. Her life was like a fairytale."

"Until it wasn't," I supplied.

Parker nodded. "Until it wasn't."

"So what happened?" Josie asked, although based on the look on her face, I suspected she knew the answer.

Parker continued. "Penelope told me that Braylon's sweet, gentle personality dramatically changed when one of the cases he was working on began to go wrong. Penelope said he was an ambitious man who liked to win, and when he realized that he might lose, he went a little crazy. She tried to offer him support, but that just seemed to enrage him. She made a comment about everyone losing sometimes, and that was the first time he hit her."

I cringed. Everyone cringed.

"She told me that he assured her that he was sorry," Parker continued. "She shared that he was so gentle and sweet and promised never to do it again. He swore that his grief over losing, combined with the substantial amount of scotch he'd consumed, had been behind his rage. He gave her flowers and bought her a diamond bracelet worth a fortune. She forgave him. She said it was fine for a while, but eventually, Braylon had another bad day, and once again, she found herself the object of his rage. As he had before, he apologized and bought her a nice gift. And as she had before, she forgave him. I guess this went on for about a year until one day, as she lay on the floor in a puddle of her own blood, she realized that she'd had enough. It was then that she began to plan a way to get away from him."

"Why didn't she just ask for a divorce?" Jemma asked.

Parker answered. "Penelope knew he'd never agree to that. She knew that she was a possession to him, an object to own and parade around to his friends. She was young and beautiful, with the exception of those times she had a black eye or split lip. She'd mentioned leaving him after one of the attacks, and he told her in no uncertain terms that he took the vow *until death do us part* seriously, and the only way she'd ever leave him was if death came into the equation, and that the death he spoke of wouldn't be his."

I put my hand on my stomach. Suddenly, I felt ill. "I guess Penelope must have found her opportunity."

Parker nodded. "She bought some cheap clothes, hair dye, scissors, and dark glasses and packed a bag that she hid. Penelope found someone who made fake IDs and not only purchased drivers licenses and passports but social security cards and credit cards as well. The credit cards were for identification only and not to be used for purchases, so she knew she'd need cash. She found a jeweler who switched out the gems in the very expensive jewelry her husband had bought her after each beating for fakes. The jeweler then bought the real gems for cash, which she stowed away as well."

"Wasn't she afraid her husband would find out about the switch?" Jemma asked.

Parker shook her head. "She admitted to me that she'd taken a bit of a risk, but she was careful, the fakes were of good quality, and by this point, Braylon didn't really pay all that much attention to her unless he needed to parade her to an event he'd been invited to attend. She felt reasonably certain that she'd be able to keep her secret, at least for a while. Once she had everything in place, she waited until he went out of town on an overnight trip, which he did at least monthly. She used some of the cash she'd stashed away to buy an old used car, drove to Napa where she rented a room in a cheap hotel, cut and colored her hair, and then traded the car she'd driven from San Francisco for a train ticket north using a fake name and ID. Once she felt she was far enough away from home, she bought another old car and took to the road. She told me that she initially landed in a small town in Montana. She knew her husband was looking for her and that she needed to keep moving."

"The guy must have known she just took off. Why would he even bother to look for her?" Josie asked.

Parker shrugged. "The guy was probably just mad that his favorite toy was gone.

"So she's been running all this time?" Jemma asked.

Parker nodded. "She said she eventually came to Gooseberry Bay because she missed the sea. She figured that our little town was far enough from San Francisco that Braylon wouldn't stumble across her and that it had been long enough since she'd taken off that he'd most likely stopped looking for her. She doesn't know how he found her. When she saw him in the bar and grill, she ran and hid in the woods. She stayed in the woods all night, and then just before sunrise, she headed back to town. The yacht was gone, so she hoped Braylon was gone as well. She cleaned up, packed a bag in case she needed to run again, and then went into work. She knew she should leave, but she was just beginning to make a life here. If Braylon had looked around, hadn't found her, and had gone, maybe she'd finally be safe for the first time in a long time."

"So how did Deputy Todd find out that Anne was Penelope?" I asked.

Parker shrugged. "I'm not sure. He didn't really say. I guess he did his research. Or maybe he received a tip. The guy had just arrived in the area. Who other than the woman who's been running from him would want to see him dead?"

"Maybe someone from the yacht," Josie said. "The crew or maybe a friend. I suppose the crew might have known Penelope from when she was married to Braylon. Maybe this crew member felt sympathy for Penelope, so they followed Braylon ashore, and then once he was alone, they killed him."

I had to admit that theory actually had merit.

"If the killer isn't a local, it's going to be hard to prove any of this at this point," Josie said.

Unfortunately, that was true. Still, the man had come into town on his fancy yacht and then walked straight through town on his way to the Rambling Rose. I was sure that people noticed him. Parker had. Maybe others had stopped to look as well. He appeared to have been shot within a few hours of stopping at the bar and grill, but a couple hours wasn't immediately. Maybe he'd gone to a bar or into a shop while he waited to make his move. Perhaps he'd shown Penelope's photo around and asked about her. Maybe someone had seen him speaking with someone about his missing wife. It was a longshot, but it seemed possible that if we dug a bit, we could dig up a clue as to what happened after he left the bar and grill and who other than Penelope might have killed him.

"Penelope is going to be arraigned tomorrow," Josie said. "I'm going to show up and offer my support."

"I plan to show as well," Parker said. "I'm going to do some additional background research on both Braylon and Penelope tonight and then write up my story after Penelope sees the judge. I suspect she'll be denied bail, but we'll see how it works out."

"If bail is set and it's reasonable, I'm going to pay it," Josie said. "I don't know Penelope well, but I know her well enough to believe her."

"Yeah, I'm in as well," I said. "Anything you need. I'm going to take a walk around town tomorrow and see if I can pick up a lead. Call me when the arraignment is over."

Parker was going to the arraignment with Josie, so Jemma volunteered to come with me. If Penelope was telling the truth, and I had no reason to believe she wasn't, then I had a feeling she was going to need all the help she could get.

Once the details were settled, Parker left, and I used the opportunity to talk to Jemma about the hard drive we'd found. I explained about the blood on the ground as well as the security system. I also explained that it was our belief that if surveillance footage existed, they were on that hard drive. She agreed to do what she could and then let me know what she found.

Once that was settled, the dogs and I headed home. I figured I'd try to get an early start tomorrow since I was supposed to show up at the community center at three. I'd noticed that the booth they'd set up on the boardwalk to sell advance tickets for the haunted house and other Halloween events had been busy all day. I had a feeling that opening night was going to be a sold-out event. The gang from the Geek Squad had been assigned the role of zombies on both Thursday and Friday nights. Not only had I been in charge of finding volunteers, but helping with the event itself Thursday and Friday evening as well.

Tossing a match on the fire I'd built earlier, I clicked on the orange lights over my mantel. I'd taken the garland Jemma had offered me, mixed it in with the lights, and added a couple candles as well. There was a large round pumpkin on my dining table, as well as several smaller gourds placed strategically around the room. The tiny cottage with the festive lights and soothing fire really did have a cozy feel.

After making a cup of tea, I curled up on the sofa with a blanket and my laptop and began my search for Willamina Krause. I knew that Warren and his PI were working on it, but finding Avery was my mission in life, so I couldn't sit back and let others do all the work. Unfortunately, Willamina had been born and raised in Germany and hadn't been seen in Germany or anywhere else for a quarter of a century, so my search results were pretty sparse.

I glanced down at the dogs, who were curled up in front of the fire. They seemed so content and peaceful, which was nice, given the fact that I felt neither at this moment. The woman I remembered from my childhood had been named Wilma. Or at least that's what I'd discovered from others once I'd begun to dig around. If Willamina was Wilma, and it seemed that she was, I had to wonder if she used the last name of Krause or if she'd changed it. I changed my search to one within the States using the name Wilma Krause but came up empty. It seemed that Wilma was involved as a friend to Marilee, so it wasn't like there would be payroll records of any sort. She hadn't been in Gooseberry Bay long, and no one either Adam or I had spoken with remembered her other than to say that she showed up a few days before Marilee left with the children. Of course, if Willamina Krause came into the States, she must have had a passport. I hadn't found one, and while she might have used a fake, it was an avenue worth exploring.

I leaned back on the sofa, picking up my teacup and taking a sip of the rapidly cooling brew. Staring into the dancing flames of the fire, I tried to let my mind rest with the image of Wilma and the details relating to the woman that I did know. Unfortunately, I didn't know a lot. Not really enough to do anything with. Still, there must be something I'd stored away in my mind that I could use to find the trail that would hopefully lead to my sister.

Setting my teacup on the table in front of me, I slid my laptop onto the table as well. I focused on the sound of the wind blowing through the trees outside the window as the flickering flame from the fireplace lulled me into a relaxed state. I let my mind wander back to the memories I did have. Playing on the patio and wanting to hide my baby birds, Marilee telling me not to get dirty, and Wilma showing up in the doorway with Avery resting on her hip. I remembered being afraid of Wilma. I remembered being uneasy around Marilee as well. Neither were around much that summer. Not like Winnie, Mr. Johnson, or Mr. Westminster. Both Mr. Westminster and Mr. Johnson were dead, and I already knew that Winnie didn't remember much other than to verify that Wilma was Willamina and that she had left the area with one of the children.

It made sense to me that if Wilma had stayed at the estate, even if only for a short time, Kingston would have inquired as to her full name. Adam and I had gone through boxes and boxes of paperwork looking for anything that would lead us to clues relating to Marilee, but we hadn't really focused on Wilma. I wondered if it might be worth our while to go back through those things to see if we could find anything specifically relating to this woman. I'd promised to help the gang find answers relating to the question of who actually killed Braylon Dario tomorrow, and then I had the haunted house tomorrow night, but maybe Adam would have some time to work with me Friday afternoon or at some point on Saturday. After picking my cell phone up, I shot off a text to ask him if and when he was available. Adam texted back to let me know that he had volunteer duty in town Friday afternoon and evening but that he would be happy to meet with me Saturday. I agreed that Saturday worked, and we set up a time.

With that settled, I got up, banked the fire, and headed off to bed. When I'd first come to Gooseberry Bay, I'd had frequent vivid dreams of my time at the house on Piney Point as a child. As I'd begun to get my answers, and as my life here in the present became fuller, those dreams had faded. Still, I wondered if exploring my memories through dreams was a good idea after all. I knew that willing myself to have a dream didn't always work, but it had worked a time or two in the past, so as I faded off to sleep, I focused my thoughts on the memories I had of Wilma and hoped my subconscious would do the rest.

Chapter 11

"The dream was so odd," I said to Jemma as I sat at her kitchen counter the following morning, waiting for her to gather her things in preparation for heading into town. Jemma had already informed me that she had a computer program she'd written working on breaking the password for the hard drive I'd given her and anticipated that she'd be in by midday. There was nothing to do at this point, she assured me, other than to wait for the program to do its thing.

"Dreams are odd. That seems to be the nature of dreams in general. What exactly happened?"

I took a sip of the coffee Jemma had given me when I'd first arrived. "As I told you before, I went to sleep with the intent in my mind to dream about Wilma. Now that we know that Marilee actually met

Wilma while she was in Italy, her role in everything that happened afterward seems more important."

"I agree." She sat down on the sofa and began pulling on socks. "Go on. You fell asleep thinking about Wilma. Then what?"

"I don't remember the whole thing, but I do remember standing in a dark hallway outside a tall, tall door. This door was like thirty feet tall, and I was just a child, so it seemed to go on forever and ever. Anyway, I'm standing outside this door in the dark hallway watching a panda talking on the phone."

"Panda?" Jemma turned, raising a brow.

I nodded. "I told you the dream was weird. Anyway, the panda wasn't a real panda. It was more like a cartoon panda or maybe a person wearing a panda costume. I remember that, in my dream, I was accepting of the fact that I was standing in this dark hallway watching a panda on the phone. The other thing that I remember was knowing that the panda was really Mr. Winchester."

"Adam's dad?"

I nodded. "I think the memory of me waking up after I'd been put to bed and sneaking down the hallway to watch as Mr. Winchester talked on the phone is a real one that actually happened. I'm not sure where the part about the panda comes in, but I do intend to ask Adam if his dad had a panda costume the next time I speak to him."

Jemma laughed. "Now, wouldn't that be something if we find out that Mr. Winchester was actually dressed up as a panda? Go on."

I smiled and continued. "Anyway, I'm standing in the dark hallway in my bare feet, watching the panda on the phone through the open door. At first, the panda is standing in front of the desk as he talks on the phone, but eventually, he walks around and sits down behind the desk. I can't remember much about the specific conversation the panda was having, but I do remember him mentioning that he needed to pick some cheese from the tree, and I remember him asking if the report had come back on Ms. Martin."

"Who's Ms. Martin?" Jemma asked.

"I really don't know, but it did occur to me that maybe Martin is the last name Wilma was using while she was here in the States. I did a search for a driver's license assigned to Wilma Martin and came up blank. I tried looking for a passport under that name, but that came up blank as well. Of course, if Wilma Martin was a fake name, then the documents she would have used to get into this country and move around once she was here might also have been fake. Then I did a general search for a reference to Wilma Martin in Washington State in nineteen ninety-five and hit pay dirt."

Jemma stood, crossed the room, and sat down next to me. "Really? What did you find?"

"Someone named Wilma Martin rented a car from the Hertz vendor at the airport in Seattle in nineteen ninety-five. The car, a dark blue Ford sedan, was never returned. The folks from Hertz tried to collect on the debt only to find that both the driver's license and the credit card that were used when the vehicle was rented were fakes."

"So Wilma must have flown in, rented a car, drove that car to Gooseberry Bay, met up with Marilee, and then used the car to leave the area with Avery."

"That's my guess. The car was reported as stolen after Wilma failed to return it, which is the piece of information I stumbled upon. Unfortunately, the vehicle was never found. I do have the VIN number and the license plate number assigned to the vehicle, but I'm sure it was dropped off at a chop shop or dumped in the ocean or some such thing."

"Wow," Jemma hugged me. "That's huge."

I hugged her back. "I'm not sure huge is the appropriate word here since we still don't know where Wilma went or what name she might have switched to after leaving here, but it is something. I called Warren and gave him the information. His PI has been doing a wonderful job finding the remnants of the trail left behind by both Wilma and Marilee."

"It sounds like Adam's dad must have had his own suspicions about what was going on," Jemma said. "If the context of the conversation you overheard is accurate, it sounds as if he was looking into the women, or at least Wilma. I wonder if he ever found anything."

I shrugged. "I really don't know, but now that we have more information, Adam and I are going to go back through the boxes of stuff left by his parents that we've marked as being relevant according to the date of the contents one more time. We plan to meet Saturday, and looking for a background check report of some sort is on the top of my list." I paused briefly before continuing. "I wish I could remember more. And I wish things were a bit clearer. Dreaming about a panda on the phone sort of makes me distrust the whole thing, although the name I remembered hearing did pan out, so maybe I'm actually onto something."

"I think you are," Jemma said, standing up and grabbing her shoulder bag. "I'm not sure where the panda comes in, but I feel like there are memories to access, and you will find the answers you need once you're able to sort things out in your mind."

"I hope so. I'm really happy here in Gooseberry Bay, and I love my cottage and my friends, but I'm not sure I'll ever be totally content unless I can find Avery and put this really odd story to rest once and for all."

Jemma locked the door before we headed out to the parking area. "Have you remembered anything else about Marilee, your dad, or Daria?"

"No. And I'm fine with that. It's obvious that my dad lied about how he came to be with me, and while I do wonder about the details, I think I've figured out enough to feel content with my mission as long as I find Avery. Sure, it would be nice to know how the whole thing with the warehouse fire comes into play, and I guess I'd like to understand why he never legally adopted me, but I had a good life. He was a great dad, and I'm grateful for that. The details are interesting, but not really all that important. But Avery. Avery is the one loose thread I can't ignore. I need to find her. I need to know that she's okay. Until I know that, I'm not sure I'll ever find real peace."

"I get it. And you know I'm here for you."

We decided to take both cars for the short drive into town. Jemma had three hours to contribute to our search, and then she really did have to get back to finish a project she'd promised to a client. I had the haunted house to get to by three, but I had more time than Jemma between now and then, so I wanted to have the option to stay in town when Jemma left if there were leads left to follow at that point.

"So, where should we start?" Jemma asked once we'd parked in the lot behind Ainsley Holloway Investigations.

"Parker saw the man come across the bay to the marina from the yacht in a dinghy. I guess let's start there. Maybe someone working at the marina saw something either at the time the man came across or after Parker had continued on."

"It's too bad Booker is in Hawaii with Tegan this week."

"It is," I agreed. "But maybe Jackson was working Monday. I say we go and ask him."

As it turned out, Jackson did remember seeing the murder victim come across the bay from the yacht to the dock.

"Yeah, I saw him. Tall guy, dark hair. Came across and tied up."

"Do you know where he went?" Jemma asked.

Jackson shook his head. I didn't talk to him, so I really have no idea. I noticed a second dinghy come across a couple hours after the first one. Different guy. Shorter. Broader shoulders. Wearing a red shirt. I'm pretty sure he was crew, while the first man looked more like an owner or guest."

"Did you see where the second man went?" Jemma asked.

"No. I wasn't really paying attention."

"Did you see when either man left?" I jumped in.

"No, the first guy came across around three or maybe three-thirty, and the second man came across around six. I got off work at six and was just locking up when he arrived. The dinghies were there when I left, but both dinghies and the yacht were gone by the time I arrived yesterday morning. I'm afraid I don't know anything more than that."

After speaking to Jackson, Jemma and I continued down the boardwalk, stopping to show Braylon's photo, which Jemma had pulled up on her cell phone, to those we passed. A few vendors remembered noticing the man arrive on the boardwalk from the yacht, but no one remembered seeing where he went once he passed their cart or booth.

"So it seems as if Braylon headed directly toward the Rambling Rose once he came ashore," I said. "We know he went inside, had coffee, and then left shortly after. Jackson verified that both dinghies and the yacht were in place when he left the marina after work. So the question is, where did the man go after he left the Rambling Rose?"

"If he was here to find Penelope, and at this point, we're only assuming that's true, then he must have gone to look for her after realizing that she wasn't at work," Jemma suggested.

"That makes sense. What doesn't make sense is how the man even knew Penelope was here. Given the fact that he headed directly to the Rambling Rose, it seems as if he not only knew she was in Gooseberry Bay, but he knew where she worked."

"I suppose someone who knew her as Penelope might have come to the area for a getaway and noticed her but decided not to approach. Maybe someone who knew the story and believed Braylon rather than Penelope and wanted to give him a heads up."

I supposed that made as much sense as anything. Still, it seemed that if Braylon was here to track his runaway wife down, he would have arrived in the area in a less flashy fashion. He must have known that if she noticed him before he noticed her, she'd run again. Showing up in his yacht and then walking down the main street running through town wasn't all that stealthy. It would have been better to have arrived in a car and then driven directly to the bar and grill.

"What if Braylon being here is a coincidence?" I asked. "What if he wasn't here to hunt down his runaway wife but for another reason altogether?"

"Like what?" Jemma asked.

I shrugged. "I don't know. The guy had friends; he had clients. He probably knew a lot of people. Maybe he had business here."

"So he just happens to come across the bay in a dinghy and then head directly to the exact bar and grill where his runaway wife works for a cup of coffee before conducting whatever bit of business he was here to conduct?"

"I know it sounds unlikely, but it is possible. Braylon didn't ask for Penelope by name. It appears that he didn't notice her in the bar and grill's back room. Josie waited on him. If he was in Gooseberry Bay to track Penelope down, it seems like, at the very least, he might have asked Josie about other staff members. He could have made something up about having been in the previous day and noticing someone he thought he knew or something like that."

Jemma frowned. "Yeah, I guess. Unless he knew she was a flight risk and didn't want to spook her. Maybe he just figured that he'd keep an eye on the place."

"If he didn't want to spook her, why arrive on the yacht?" I asked for the second time.

Jemma admitted that part didn't make sense and while the odds of this guy randomly showing up in the very bar and grill where his ex-wife worked were astronomical, it wasn't impossible that wasn't exactly what had happened. The question was if he wasn't here looking for Penelope, why was he here?

"Do we know if the yacht was owned by Braylon?" I asked, trying to recall the conversation we'd had with Parker.

"I can't remember if Parker ever said. I know it was her opinion that the man who came over didn't own the vessel, but I'm not sure anyone ever followed up on it."

"We should try to find that out," I suggested. I paused and looked around. "I guess we should try to figure out where the man went after leaving the Rambling Rose too. No one we've spoken to remembers seeing him, so he may have taken a different route after leaving the bar and grill than the one he took on the way there."

"There are a couple bars on Second Street," Jemma pointed out. "I realize the guy had just had coffee, but maybe he decided he needed something stronger."

"Not if he actually was in town to conduct business." I furrowed my brow. "It seems that if he was here on business, he would have needed a car. Unless, of course, the business he was here to conduct was with one of the merchants in this immediate area."

"Maybe he called for a car. I suppose Deputy Todd has the guy's cell phone, but I might be able to hack into his phone records. Of course, he most likely has both a personal and business cell phone. I don't have his number, but I have his name and occupation. I'm sure I can figure it out." She glanced at her watch. "I don't have a lot of time right now, but I can work on it once I finish up the job I promised my client would be ready today."

I'd hoped we'd find a smoking gun during our stroll up and down Main Street chatting with folks, but we really hadn't discovered anything we hadn't already known. I knew that sometimes these things took time, and I simply needed to be patient until the answers revealed themselves, but I felt so bad for Penelope sitting alone in jail, and I really did want to solve this case sooner rather than later. Jemma and I decided to continue down the road stopping to ask those we encountered if they'd noticed the man who'd arrived on the yacht. I knew that simply wandering around talking to people wasn't the most effective investigative tactic, but we really didn't have a lot to go on at this point.

By the time Jemma announced that she needed to get back to the cottage, it was past the lunch hour, so we parted ways. I spoke to a few more people and then decided to hang it up for now as well. As I walked toward my office, I found myself wondering if Penelope had been arraigned yet. I supposed I'd call Josie or Parker for an update once I arrived at my office. I knew that both women planned to attend the arraignment to show their support.

After entering my office, I checked my messages and then called Parker.

"Have you heard anything?" I asked after she picked up.

"I'm at the courthouse now. Court just resumed after lunch. I think Penelope will be up within the next half hour."

"Fingers crossed," I said.

"Yeah, me too. I have to go. I'll call you when we finish up here."

After I hung up, I debated what to do. I could rest up and then go back out and continue to canvas the area, but I felt like my search was too unfocused to really amount to much. I was hungry since I hadn't eaten breakfast, and it was after lunchtime now, so I decided to grab a sandwich. I'd need to head over to the community center in a little more than an hour, but I supposed I had time to get some paperwork done in the meantime. I turned my computer on and finished off my sandwich while I waited for it to boot up. After tossing the sandwich wrapper and my napkin into the wastebasket, I opened my inbox. Most of the emails I'd received since the last time I'd checked were garbage, but there were a few emails that deserved a thorough read-through. I was in the middle of answering one from a former client when Parker called.

"So?" I asked as soon as I answered.

"The arraignment is over. Penelope pled not guilty, but the judge denied bail as we suspected he would. I guess I get it. Penelope doesn't have any ties to the town or the community. She doesn't really have ties anywhere."

"Is there any actual evidence that Penelope killed this man?" I asked.

"No. But the district attorney has made a case that she had motive and opportunity. I guess at this point, all we can do is hope that either we catch the real bad guy or her attorney comes up with something to cast doubt on the whole thing."

I blew out a breath. "Anything else?"

"Actually, yes. It turns out that Deputy Todd is in a generous mood today. Not only did he tell me that the blood found at Professor Beklund's place did turn out to be human, but he also shared that the blood belonged to Braylon Dario."

I raised a brow even though Parker couldn't see me. "Really? I wasn't expecting that. In fact, I was expecting to find that the blood belonged to Beklund. I'm glad to hear that I was wrong about that." After a brief pause, I continued. "You know, if the blood out at Beklund's place belongs to Dario, that suggests that it was Beklund and not Penelope who might have shot him."

"I agree. I mentioned that to Todd, but then he pointed out that you and the Geek Squad have been squawking for days that Beklund was missing long before Dario was killed. It's Todd's opinion that Dario went out to Beklund's place to speak to the man, that Penelope followed him, and shot him in the back as he approached the cabin."

I supposed that it could have happened that way, but I sort of doubted it especially given the fact that Penelope didn't own a car and the cabin was quite a ways out of town.

"Why would Dario go out to Beklund's property in the first place?" I asked. The guy was an attorney, but Beklund didn't seem like the sort of client he'd take on.

"The yacht Braylon Dario arrived on belongs to Intelligene. Todd believes, and I agree, that Ronald Evington is a client of either Dario or the firm he works for and that Dario had gone to speak to Beklund on his behalf."

"So Evington was interested in whatever Beklund found as Beklund had indicated he would be," I realized.

"It appears he may have been, although Todd didn't go into any detail other than to say that it appeared that Dario had gone to speak to the professor, who, as far as he's concerned, wasn't home at the time of the visit. Todd is certain that while Dario was at the property when he was shot, it was Penelope who caught up with him and ended his life."

"So Todd isn't looking for Beklund at all?"

"It didn't seem like it. In fact, it seemed clear that the guy is really invested in nailing Penelope for Braylon's death. To be honest, I'm not sure Todd's going to put much effort into tracking Beklund down. I suspect that in his mind, the presence of the absent-minded professor will just muddy what he seems to think is an open and shut case."

It figured that Todd would be more interested in closing the case than finding the actual killer. Not that I wanted Bek to be the killer. If he was, I was sure the Geek Squad would be devastated. Still, in my mind, given what I knew at this point, it really did appear that he was as strong a suspect as anyone was.

"Listen," Parker said. "I need to go. I'll catch up with you this evening if you still plan to show up at Jemma and Josie's."

"I'll be there," I promised and then hung up. A quick glance at the clock indicated that I should head to the community center to meet my volunteers. The problem was that I really had no idea what I was going to tell the five volunteers who'd hired me to find their friend. Not only had I not found him, but now I had news that the man might actually turn out to be a killer.

Chapter 12

I had to admit that the decorating committee had done a terrific job converting the community center into an authentic-looking haunted house. Not only was the interior of the building completely transformed to include dark spaces, false walls, and blind alleyways, but a local contractor had built a false front for the building, creating the illusion of a dilapidated old house with sagging balconies and cracked windows. The color scheme for the exterior was dirty gray with hints of black and off-white accents, and there were varying tones of each color to give depth and authenticity to the painting, and from a distance, the building gave off a really spooky vibe. The line was already extensive, beginning at the closed front doors and extending around the building before looping around once again. I wasn't sure how many ticket holders they planned to let in at a time, but based on the line already formed, if they didn't cut it off soon, they'd never get everyone through before the event was scheduled to end for the evening.

I'd taken a quick peek inside, although I hadn't taken the time to walk through the eight separate rooms that had been created. I knew that when you first entered the building, you'd find a long dark hallway that would take the ticket holder into the main room where the mood would be set, and access to the other seven rooms would be provided.

The fifteen volunteers I'd recruited for the zombie role had been divided into three groups of five. Each group had been asked to sign up for two shifts over the course of the four-day event. On Thursday and Friday, the haunted house was open from five to ten. On Saturday, a mild kiddie version of the event was offered from noon to five, and then after an hour break, the high thrills and chills adult version was live from six to ten. Sunday featured a return to the kiddie version from ten a.m. to two p.m., with clean-up beginning immediately after the last ticket holder departed.

I knew the Geek Squad had volunteered for both Thursday and Friday night. I guess they didn't want their volunteer duties spilling into their weekend. Not that I blamed them. I'd protected my weekends as well when I was their age, refusing to schedule any sort of lessons, tutoring, or school-related activities during my two days of rest. Of course, I had played soccer, and that had been held on Saturdays. And once I'd entered high school, I'd joined the track team, and there were more early morning Saturday meets than I would have preferred. Still, in general, I preferred Saturdays to be a lazy day when I could arrange it.

"Hey, guys," I said to the group, who were already dressed and assembled when I arrived. "You look so awesome. Very authentic and fairly terrifying."

"The guys and I dress up for Comic-Con sometimes, so we have a collection of the best makeup," Cosmo said. "Honestly, I wasn't thrilled with this assignment in the beginning, but now that we're here, I'm really into it."

"Yeah," Skeet agreed. "I think this might actually be fun."

I hoped the teens would have a good time. I almost felt like I was taking advantage of them since they'd helped me to fill my quota of volunteers, and I hadn't come up with much at all about their missing friend. I thought about bringing up the news that Braylon Dario had been shot and killed out at Bek's place but decided that news could wait. They really seemed into their roles as zombies, and I didn't want to do anything to ruin the fun they were having.

"It looks like all the major monsters are represented," I said, looking around the room at the zombies, vampires, werewolves, witches, and ghosts.

"One of the guys who did this last year told me they have different themes each year," Ape commented. "Last year, everyone dressed as a slasher of one sort or another. My friend was Freddy

Krueger. This year, the theme is the monster next door, so all the monsters featured started off as human but have been turned into something else."

"Clever."

"I thought so," Ape agreed.

"Hope wants us to gather in the room being used for the actors no later than three-thirty," Phoenix said, glancing around the room as if looking for a wall clock. "I don't want to be late, but before we head in, do you have any news?"

"I do have a few things, but I'm still waiting for some return calls before I know anything for certain. Why don't we plan to meet up tomorrow so we can really go over things. I know you're doing another volunteer shift tomorrow. Would you have time to meet before that?"

The kids agreed that they could meet me at my office at two o'clock if that worked for me. I told them it did. I hoped to have answers for them by the time we met.

Once the teens had headed to the room where they'd been assigned to gather, I headed toward the ticket booth to see if there was anyone around who knew what needed to be done. Since I planned to meet up with Parker and the roommates later this afternoon, I didn't want to get pulled into anything that would require a significant time commitment, but I had a couple hours until I needed to head back to the peninsula and wanted to do what I could if help was needed.

"Wow, the line to get in already wraps around the building," I said as I moseyed up to where two women were selling tickets.

"The line is crazy every year," one of the women replied. "Especially for opening night. The haunted house is slightly different each year, so the real hardcore spook seekers want to go through first before anyone can ruin it for them."

"I heard about the change in theme from year to year. That seems like a good marketing strategy."

"Oh, it is. We've had kids lining up since before noon," the second volunteer provided.

"Shouldn't they have been at school at that time of the day?" I asked.

"They should have been," the woman commented. "But cutting class on opening day certainly isn't unheard of." She handed a pretty young girl with long black hair the four tickets she'd paid for and then glanced at the next person in line. "Have you been to one of our haunted houses?" she asked.

"No," I answered as the woman handed a man with three children four tickets. "I moved to Gooseberry Bay on Halloween day last year, so this will be my first time enjoying the annual festivities. I only have a couple hours to donate to the cause today, but I'm happy to help while I can if you need anything."

"Actually," the first woman I'd spoken to smiled as she spoke, "if you could take over here for maybe an hour, that would help a lot. I'm really supposed to be helping with the food vendors, but they were short help in the ticket booth, so I came over to help out with that."

"I'd be happy to fill in," I said, standing aside so the woman could come out of the booth, allowing me access to go in. It was tight in the partially enclosed structure but adequate for two people to stand.

"Hi," I said to the second woman after the first woman left. "I'm Ainsley."

"Clara."

"I'm happy to meet you, Clara. Is there anything specific I should know?"

"Just that the adult tickets are ten dollars, teens between twelve and eighteen are eight, students with a student ID can get in for five, and kids between five and eleven are three. Kids under five are free if they go in with a paid adult, although if you see someone with a child under five, you should suggest they come back Saturday afternoon or Sunday morning. The event held in the evenings isn't geared toward the little ones."

Once I understood the pricing structure, I greeted my first customer. I had to admit there was an energy that had me wishing I had time to hang out and partake in the festivities. I was meeting with the Geek Squad after school tomorrow, but since they had a volunteer shift at three, unless I was busy with the Braylon Dario case, I should have time to come by right around opening time.

"So you're that new PI in town," Clara said after a moment of silence.

"Yes. I opened my business this past winter."

"I noticed the sign painted on your window. You're next to Hair Affair."

I nodded.

"Peggy is such a kick," Clara said. "She's been doing my hair for years now, and I swear every time I go in for a trim or root touch up, I come away with a belly ache from all the laughing."

I smiled. "Peggy does have a unique way about her. And she's been so supportive. Ella too," I referred to the second hairdresser.

Clara turned and glanced in my direction. "I guess with all that pretty blond hair, you don't have much need of a hairdresser."

"No," I agreed. "Not really. I did go in over the summer and had Ella give me a trim, but with long hair all one length, I don't have a lot of regular maintenance."

"Did Ella mention that her sister, Gwen, is moving to the area after the first of the year?" Clara asked.

"No." I handed the woman at the front of the line her change after she'd bought tickets for five teens and four elementary-aged boys. "Is Gwen the sister who lives in Vermont?"

"No. That's Pam. Gwen is in the Army. I guess she's getting out around the holidays. Gwen isn't sure what she wants to do with the new phase of her life, so after she heads home and spends some time with her parents, she's going to live with Ella and work on a plan."

"It's nice that Ella has an extra bedroom."

"It really is. And Ella is so sweet to let her sister use it."

"Are Ella and Gwen close?" I asked.

Clara paused as the line shifted once again. "I'm not sure. I know there's an age difference, but that isn't always important."

I agreed with Clara's assessment that age wasn't necessarily a key factor when it came to relationships within family units. The conversation paused as the next four women in line each purchased multiple tickets for multiple age groups for multiple days, which had me scrambling to keep everything straight. It seemed that the women were all together. If I had to guess, they were friends or neighbors who'd banned together to buy tickets for the entire neighborhood.

"I guess you heard about that man they found dead in the bay," Clara said once things slowed down a bit.

"I did. Did you know him?" I figured she didn't, but I also figured that by asking, I was opening the door for her to share anything she might have heard about the murder. After working with Clara for an hour, it seemed evident that she'd lived in the area for a long time and knew a lot of people.

"No, I didn't know him. I understand he's from out of the area. My neighbor, Jean, told me that the guy showed up on that big yacht that was anchored in the bay. Not sure why he was here, but I did hear that he was dead by morning."

"Really?" I adjusted my facial expression to show just the right amount of interest. "Did you hear what happened?"

She shrugged. "There are a lot of rumors going around. I'm not sure that anyone actually knows anything at this point. Initially, I heard the guy had drowned, but then I heard he was shot. I'm not sure which, if either, is true."

"Any idea why he was here in the first place?" I smiled as the two little boys who couldn't be any older than six or seven reached up with a wad of bills clutched in their hands. I'd hoped they were buying tickets for the kiddie event, but as it turned out, they planned to go through the haunted house tonight with the swarms of teens and adults who'd already shown up.

"I'm not sure why the man was here," Clara said. "It seems odd to me that the guy came to Gooseberry Bay on that big yacht, and then it left at some point during the overnight hours even though the man wasn't back on account of him being dead and all. You'd think that if the guy didn't return, the crew would have gone looking for him instead of taking off the way they did.

I supposed that was odd. I wondered who else might have been on board. I was about to ask Clara if she'd heard anything about the size of the crew or the number of passengers on board when the woman I'd relieved so she could check on the food vendors came back, apologizing for taking longer than she'd planned. A quick glance at my watch confirmed that I'd been selling tickets for close to two hours. I supposed being late for the dinner and strategy session I'd planned to attend wasn't the end of the world, but I did hope that the group wasn't sitting around waiting for me.

I said goodbye to each woman, grabbed my things, and then headed toward the cottages. As I passed the very southern end of the bay, the conversation I'd just had played through my mind. Clara hadn't been wrong when she said it was odd that the yacht left without Dario even if he hadn't returned to the yacht at the designated time. Surely the first instinct of the crew would be to look for the guy and report him as missing if he hadn't been found. But to simply pull up anchor and leave even though the man hadn't returned really didn't make a lick of sense. Unless, of course, it was someone from the yacht who'd killed him.

Chapter 13

By the time I made it back to the peninsula, everyone had gathered at Jemma and Josie's. I asked what I'd missed, and they informed me that Parker had just arrived and Josie had been busy making dinner, so they hadn't really discussed anything.

"Before we get too far into this and I forget to bring this up, I managed to crack the password for the hard drive you brought mc from Beklund's property," Jemma informed us.

I smiled. "Really? That's great."

"Did you find anything?" Parker asked.

"Sort of," Jemma answered. "I've managed to isolate the surveillance footage for the evening Braylon Dario died." Jemma pulled an image up on her computer screen, which she then sent to the television screen so that everyone could see it. "As you can see, Dario comes out of the woods here." She pointed toward the screen as a man wearing khaki pants and a light blue polo shirt appeared. "He appears to be alone, and he appears to know exactly where he's going," she continued. "When he emerges from the woods, there's no hesitation. He doesn't stop to look around to get his bearings or to scout things out. He just continues forward."

We all watched as the man continued across the clearing toward the cabin. He climbed the front stairs and then knocked on the door. When there was no answer, he knocked again. The recording didn't have audio, but it appeared he called out. He knocked one last time, and then he came down the stairs. He took maybe ten steps away from the cabin and then turned around and looked back toward the structure.

"Why'd he turn back?" Parker asked.

"I'm not sure," Jemma paused the recording and answered. "He may have heard something. This next part is the important part."

She restarted the recording. Dario continued to stand still, looking at the cabin for maybe five seconds, and then he fell to the ground.

Everyone gasped.

"This is where he must have been shot," I said. "Did anyone see the shooter?"

Everyone admitted that they hadn't. The shot had come from the cover of the woods. The evening was fading, so the light was compromised.

"I've re-watched this footage dozens of times," Jemma said. "The shooter is hidden in the trees. At no point does he or she make an appearance until much later."

"Much later?" I asked.

Jemma fast-forwarded. By the time she slowed the recording, the sky was totally dark. Dario was still lying on the ground where he'd fallen, although due to the darkness of the night, you could barely see him. What we did see, after a time, was a figure dressed in all black. The figure walked over to Dario, slung his dead body over one shoulder, and headed back into the forest.

"Okay, there is no way that was Penelope," Josie said. "I bet that girl doesn't weigh more than a hundred pounds soaking wet."

"I agree," Parker said. "There is no way the person who came back for Dario was Penelope."

"So we can use this to get her set free," Josie popped in again.

"Maybe and maybe not," I said. "The person who came for the body was obviously not Penelope, but we never see the face of the shooter or the person who took the body away. If the district attorney is really invested in making Penelope the fall guy for Dario's murder, he can argue that she shot the man and then went for help to move the body."

"Why was the body moved?" Parker asked. "No one was around. The only person who had anything to lose by having the body found where the murder occurred is Ivan Beklund."

"Maybe Beklund was the shooter," I said. "He obviously didn't come from the cabin, but what if he was in the bunker when Dario arrived. Maybe he has a monitor hooked up in the bunker as well as the cabin. Maybe he knew that Dario worked for Evington, and he figured he was there to steal his equations, so he snuck around through the woods and shot him."

"Beklund would know about the cameras, so he'd know to avoid them," Jemma said. "It fits that if he did shoot the man from the cover of the woods, he would have waited until dark and then returned to get rid of the body."

"Why not just turn the cameras off?" Josie asked.

"Maybe he suspected that the recordings might come into play at some point and knew it would be suspicious if there was missing footage," I said.

"Yeah, but why not just erase the entire recording?" Jemma said. "In fact, he could have erased all the recordings, and then if he was asked for them, he could say that he didn't keep recordings."

I let out a slow breath. "Good point. It does seem that the shooter is someone other than Beklund. But if someone other than Beklund was the killer, and we are pretty sure it wasn't Penelope, then who was it? And why? The victim didn't live in town. Who would even be around to want him dead?"

No one responded. I imagined because no one had a clue as to who would have wanted to kill the man.

"How did Dario get out to the cabin?" I asked. I looked at Jemma. "He came over from the yacht, so he didn't have a car. Did you ever get into the man's phone records?"

"No, but I did call around to the local cab and rideshare companies, and I was able to determine that a yellow cab driver named Martin Valentine picked Dario up from the marina Monday at six-ten and took him out to the property. Martin told me he offered to wait if Dario needed a return ride, but Dario told him that he was expected and wouldn't need a ride back. He then headed off into the woods."

Okay, the timing seemed right given the position of the sun on the recording. "So Dario shows up, heads to the cabin, and is shot."

"Given the fact that Dario sent the driver away, should we assume that Dario had reason to expect Bek to be there?" Parker asked. "Or was he simply taking a chance that he would be? I guess if the outcome of his visit was unknown, he might not have wanted the driver to wait."

"Is it possible that Dario had spoken to Bek before heading out to the property and had reason to assume he'd be expected?"

"Maybe," Parker agreed. "Which might explain why Bek was waiting for him with a gun."

"I feel like there's a big hole in whichever theory we decide on," I said. "If the killer was someone other than Bek, why would they move the body? The place the man fell is more isolated than the place where the body was found. Why not just leave it there? Someone would have eventually found it, so I can't think of a single reason to go to all the trouble to haul it through the woods back to a vehicle and then dump it in the bay unless Bek is the killer and wanted to try to cover up what he'd done. But if that were true, why wouldn't he simply erase the surveillance footage, as Jemma pointed out? It makes no sense that he kept the recordings."

"Could the person with the dark clothes in the recording even be Bek?" Josie asked. "Do you have any idea how tall he is or what sort of body build he has?"

"Not really," I answered. "The gang from the Geek Squad would know. They're volunteering at the haunted house tonight, but I can call them later."

"Professor Beklund looks to be tall but not necessarily built," Jemma said.

I looked toward her. "You've met Bek?"

"No, but I've been able to observe him coming and going and moving around the property on the surveillance footage."

"How far back do the recordings go?" I wondered.

"Four weeks."

"And when was the last time Bek was seen on any of the recordings?" I asked.

"October fifteenth. For several days before that, Bek had been carrying boxes from the cabin to a location in the woods. I guess he must have been going to the bunker. As far as I can tell, the trip he made to the bunker on the fifteenth is the last trip he made. I never noticed him come back to the cabin. I guess there could be an entrance around the back that I'm not aware of."

"Doesn't it seem odd to you that a murder occurred on Bek's property, and he never showed up to check on things?" Josie asked. "I mean, even if the guy was in the bunker and hadn't actually seen what had occurred, he would still have heard the gunshot."

"Unless he really isn't there," I said.

We all agreed that it was a possibility that Bek was no longer in residence on his property, but if he wasn't in the bunker, then where was he? His car never seemed to have left its parking space. I supposed we could explore the idea of cabs and rideshare companies a bit more.

"So, what do we do now?" Jemma asked. "Do we turn this over to Deputy Todd?"

"I say we turn a copy of the recording over to Todd," Parker said. "As much as I don't trust him, he is a cop, and it seems wrong to keep this from him. Besides, it might be enough to get him to take another look at Penelope. He'll be able to see for himself that she isn't the one who showed up and carried the man away."

"But we'll keep the original in the event of tampering," I said.

Parker nodded. "Exactly."

Jemma made a copy of the surveillance recording that Parker offered to take to Deputy Todd. At this point, there wasn't a lot we could do, so I grabbed my dogs and headed back to my cottage. I'd planned to work on the mystery of Wilma and my missing sister, but once I made a fire and sat down on the sofa, I promptly fell asleep. By the time I awoke, it was the middle of the night, so after checking the fire, I headed to bed.

Chapter 14

When I awoke the following morning, I had a feeling that hadn't quite worked itself out the previous evening. I'd planned to take a run, but instead, I got up and headed over to the roommates' cottage. Josie had the breakfast shift, so she'd already headed off to work, but Jemma was still sitting around in her pajamas drinking coffee.

"Ainsley? Is everything okay?" Jemma asked, probably wondering why I was bothering her at the crack of dawn.

"Everything's fine," I said. "I woke up this morning and realized that I might know who the person moving the body in the surveillance footage is. I hoped I could take another look."

She stepped aside. "Sure. Come on in. I'll pull it up on the monitor. There's coffee in the kitchen if you'd like some."

"I would. Thank you."

Once Jemma pulled the surveillance footage up, I asked her to pause the recording when the person in the black clothes arrived. As I remembered, whoever it was must have known about the cameras since the man in black was careful to hide his face, but there was something about the walk that seemed familiar. Jemma slowly proceeded through the frames as the man came into the clearing from the woods, walked over to the body, slung him over his shoulder, and then headed back through the woods.

"What do you see?" Jemma asked.

"The person in the recording looks a bit like Skeet."

"Skeet? The kid who was here the other night?"

I nodded. "The idea that Skeet would move the body to help Professor Beklund if Beklund is indeed the killer is an idea that fits. Skeet is all but an orphan. His mother is dead, and his father is in jail. The first day we met, he told me that his uncle is his legal guardian. He also told me that the man likes to drink and gamble and is never around. It sounded as if the poor kid really is on his own. And it has seemed since the beginning that of the five Geek Squad members, he's the one who's the closest to Bek." I paused to take a breath. "He said he first met Bek when he was just eleven and that they really hit it off and continued to stay in touch. After Bek moved from

Seattle to the cabin, Skeet became a frequent visitor. Eventually, he introduced Bek to Ape and then the others."

"So Skeet and Bek are close?"

I nodded. "Restart the recording and run it through again."

Jemma did as I requested.

"So, what exactly are you saying?" Jemma asked. "Do you think Skeet shot and killed Dario in order to protect Bek, or do you think Bek shot Dario and Skeet came by later and helped clean things up?"

"I'm not sure," I admitted.

Jemma paused the recording at the point where the man in black bends over to pick up the body.

"I just can't tell for sure," I said, really looking at the recording. "I'd say that based on body type and the approximate height, the person in the recording could be Skeet. However, the man in the recording wore all black, and when the kids and I went out to Beklund's property Monday, Skeet was wearing blue jeans, a t-shirt, and an orange hoodie. If he is the person on the recording, he changed first."

"Does the timeline even work for Skeet to be the killer?" Jemma asked. "I know you went out to Bek's property to have a look around Monday. What time was that?"

I paused to think about this. "The Geek Squad and I arrived at Bek's around four-thirty. There was no body at that point, which there wouldn't be since

Dario didn't arrive at the property until close to six-thirty. So yes, in answer to your question, Skeet could have dropped his friends off after we'd been out to the property, and then he could have doubled back around and killed Dario. In this scenario, he must have gone home and changed into black clothing and then returned to the property to remove the body after it was completely dark."

Jemma sat back on the sofa, her legs crossed under her body. "Okay, so you first met the Geek Squad members at your office Monday afternoon. You all went to check out the cabin together. Bek didn't answer the door, but you let yourselves in to look around. At this point, you didn't know about the bunker."

I nodded. "That's correct. We didn't learn about the existence of the bunker until Wednesday after I spoke to the real estate agent who'd sold Bek the property."

"And the surveillance cameras? You brought me the hard drive Wednesday as well. Did you know about the cameras before that?"

I nodded. "We first discovered the cameras when we went back Tuesday. We didn't feel right about taking the hard drive at that point, so we left it behind. Then we went back to the cabin Wednesday after I'd spoken to the real estate agent. It was then that Skeet decided to go ahead and grab the hard drive. I wasn't sure it was the right thing to do, but I guess I figured Todd might take it himself, and I wanted to have a look before he confiscated it."

"Did Skeet seem to know about the cameras before Tuesday when you went back and found the exterior units?" Jemma wondered.

"No. At least if he did, he didn't let on." I tried to think back. "I can't remember who said what exactly, but at the point when the five Geek Squad members and I headed out to the property Tuesday, none of the five admitted to knowing the cameras were there."

Jemma glanced up at the screen. "So given the fact that this footage was recorded Monday, and it appears the man is intentionally avoiding the cameras, the man in the recording can't be Skeet."

I frowned. "Yeah. Maybe. But I still think it looks like Skeet." I paused to think this through. "Skeet is a smart guy. He wants to be an engineer. When the group first offered to do something for me in exchange for my taking on their case and looking for Beklund, Skeet offered to help me with a security system. Skeet knew Beklund first. He seemed to visit often. It really doesn't track for me that in all the years he's been visiting the man, Skeet never noticed the cameras. Sure, they were well hidden, but still."

"So do you think Skeet knew about the cameras but pretended not to when it was brought up?"

I shrugged.

"Why?" Jemma asked.

"If he is the one on the camera, he might have suspected that a recording existed. Maybe he didn't want to draw attention to himself, so he went along with the others." I paused and tried to think back to the events of the past week. "Now that I think about it, while Skeet went along with us when we went back to look for the cameras, he really didn't help much. When the cameras were found, he was the one to suggest that they provided surveillance in real-time but probably didn't keep a record of any sort."

"I guess you should talk to him," Jemma suggested. "Probably alone."

I nodded. "Yeah. I was thinking the same thing. I have Skeet's cell phone number. I'll text him and ask him to drop by the office either during his lunch break or maybe a free period." I got up from where I was sitting. "Thanks, Jemma. I'm sorry to have disturbed you so early."

"No problem. I'm working from home today. If you don't want to take the dogs into town, drop them off on your way out."

"I will. And thanks again."

By the time I'd returned to my cottage, showered and dressed, taken the dogs for a quick walk, dropped them at Jemma's, and then made it into town, it was midmorning. When I pulled up to my office, I noticed that Skeet was sitting on the bench in front. I pulled over and waved. "I was just thinking about you."

He smiled a little half-smile that presented as more of a grimace. "Can we talk?"

"Sure." I grabbed my key and opened the door. "Come on in."

He followed me inside, and I offered him a seat. "So what's on your mind?"

He paused, swallowed hard, and then answered. "When I was at the haunted house last night, I heard some people talking about the waitress that was arrested for the death of the man they found in the bay. Until that point, I hadn't realized that anyone had been arrested."

"Do you know Anne?" I asked, wanting to keep the conversation flowing. I hoped he'd tell me what had happened on his own without my having to ask.

"No. I've never met her, but I asked around, and I realized I knew who she was. Anyway, the story being circulated is that the waitress killed the man from the yacht because he was her ex-husband and that she'd been on the run from him. Everyone I spoke to seemed convinced that she was probably guilty, but I know she isn't."

"Go on," I encouraged when he stopped talking. "How do you know Anne isn't guilty?"

"Because I know who did it. At least, I think I do." He swallowed hard again. This time I just waited. Eventually, he began to speak again. "After we went out to Bek's place Monday, I went back after I dropped everyone off. I hoped that if Bek was around but just hiding for some reason, he might show up once it was dark. I wanted to see for myself if there was any sign of movement after dark, so I went home and dressed in all black, figuring that I could sneak around and maybe avoid the cameras if Bek was watching."

"So you did know about the cameras at that point," I confirmed.

He nodded. "I pretended not to when it came up since given everything else, it seemed the best thing to do."

"Okay. Go on. You wanted to sneak back to the property after dark to see if Bek would show up. Then what happened?"

"When I arrived at the property, I saw a man lying in the meadow in front of the cabin. I could see he was dead. Or at least he looked to be dead. I slowly walked over to the body, being careful to keep my face lowered while I looked. When I saw who it was, I knew Bek must have shot him."

"So you recognized Braylon Dario?"

Skeet nodded. "He'd come around before to talk to Bek when I was there. He worked for Evington. He was his attorney, I think. I didn't know the man's name, but I recognized him as the man Bek had spoken to briefly and then sent away. It was after this that Bek started to really flip out."

I wanted to know how long ago it had been that Dario had first visited Bek, but I didn't want to interrupt the more important story, so I zipped my lip and waited for Skeet to continue.

"Anyway, once I saw the body, I knew I needed to hide it. If the body was found out at Bek's place, everyone would know that Bek killed the man. I didn't want him to go to jail, so I took the body down to the bay, rowed out toward the middle in my kayak, and dumped it. Then I came back with a shovel and a rake and buried the blood beneath a clean cover of dirt. I hoped that would be that. I hoped the fish would get the body, and no one would ever know what happened, but I guess I didn't take the body out far enough, and it washed onto the shore."

Okay, so far, all of this fit my theory. "So do you know for certain that Bek killed this man? Have you spoken to Bek?"

"No. But the guy was dead on Bek's property, just feet from his cabin. Who else would shoot him? At first, I wasn't sure where Bek was, but after finding the bunker, I'm convinced he's hanging out there. I went back again last night after my shift at the haunted house was over, but Bek wasn't there. At least he wasn't at the cabin. I tried to get into the bunker but wasn't able to. Bek must be hiding inside. I'm not sure why he won't let me in. The two of us are friends. But despite the fact that I knocked and called out, he never opened the door."

I sat back in my chair. I couldn't help but notice a single tear hovering on Skeet's cheek. I realized that Bek was probably a father figure to the boy. It took a lot of courage for him to come and tell me what he'd done. After a moment, he continued. "I don't want Bek to go to jail for killing the man who was after his work, and I don't want to go to jail for trying to hide the body, but I also don't want that waitress to be in jail for killing the man when I know she didn't do it."

"We'll need to tell Deputy Todd what you just told me."

He bowed his head. "I know. And I'm willing to. I wanted to tell you first since you've been trying so hard to help us." He made a sound much like a snort.

"Everyone said I was going to end up in jail one day just like my loser father. I knew they were wrong, but as it turns out, I guess they were right."

My heart physically hurt with that one.

"I'm going to call my friend, Adam Winchester. He can hook you up with a really good attorney. Once that's done, we'll talk to Todd together."

He nodded but didn't say anything.

I called Adam and explained what was going on. He told me to wait at my office until he could call his attorney friend and get his advice. Neither Skeet nor I had eaten, so I walked down the street and got us takeout. By the time we finished eating, Adam and the attorney he'd told me about had arrived. The attorney spoke to Skeet, and then the attorney called Deputy Todd. Deputy Todd agreed to hear Skeet out before arresting him, so the attorney and Skeet headed across town to the sheriff's office.

"What do you think is going to happen?" I asked Adam after Skeet left with the attorney.

"I'm sure Skeet will be arrested, but I'm equally sure that Carson will work out a deal of some sort given the fact that Skeet is cooperating."

"Do you think they'll let Penelope go?"

Adam shrugged. "I'm not sure. Skeet moved Dario's body since he assumed that his friend, Bek, had killed the man, but Skeet didn't actually see Bek shoot Dario. It's my opinion that Todd won't release Penelope until he has a viable suspect in custody."

Chapter 15

By the time noon rolled around, Adam had called to let me know that Skeet had been booked and released in his care. Skeet's uncle, who was acting as his guardian, was nowhere to be found, and since Skeet was a minor, they couldn't release him on his own recognizance. Usually, they wouldn't release a minor into the custody of a non-relative, but Adam was well known in the community, so when he agreed to stand in and accept temporary custody, everyone went along with it.

Before being released to Adam, Skeet had taken Deputy Todd out to the cabin and let him inside. As predicted, they hadn't found anything, and they'd been unable to get into the bunker, so Todd asked for a warrant allowing his men to enter forcefully.

Once accessed, they found the underground room was stuffed full of whiteboards. Each whiteboard seemed to feature a complicated equation. I knew Skeet had been hoping that his friend had been hiding out in the bunker. Skeet was disappointed that there was no sign that Bek, or anyone, had been staying there.

The question was if Bek hadn't been inside the bunker this whole time, where had he been?

Penelope was still in custody since Todd had no proof other than the opinion of Skeet that Bek had killed Dario. Carson had offered to do what he could to facilitate her release, but he didn't think anything would happen today. I really wanted to speak to Penelope personally, so I asked Adam if Carson would be able to arrange for a visit. He said he thought that would be possible and that he'd ask and call me back. I had my two o'clock meeting with the Geek Squad, who by this point must be wondering why Skeet had never shown up at school, so I asked Adam to try to make the visit with Penelope at three or later if possible.

I had to admit to being nervous about my meeting with the Geek Squad. I'd hoped that Skeet would be allowed to attend the meeting, but Carson felt that for the time being, Skeet was better off hanging out with Adam at the house on Piney Point rather than returning to his everyday life. Skeet seemed thrilled with the chance to explore Adam's extensive library, and Adam seemed happy for the company. I was glad the judge had allowed Skeet to go home with Adam. I think that was going to make things easier on everyone.

"Skeet never showed at school," Phoenix said the minute she walked through the door with Ape, Chip, and Cosmo following behind her.

"Yes, I know. Why don't you all have a seat, and I'll fill you in."

I spent the next fifteen minutes sharing everything that had happened since I'd arrived at work to find Skeet sitting at my doorstep.

"So Skeet hid the body?" Phoenix asked.

I'd said as much and had confirmed that fact at least twice, but she seemed stuck in her disbelief.

"Yes. It was and still is Skeet's belief that Bek is the one who shot Dario. Skeet thought he was helping his friend by moving the body."

"Do *you* think Bek killed this man?" Cosmo asked.

I paused briefly before responding. "Honestly, I'm not sure. It does seem evident that Bek believed his work was in danger, and since he mentioned Evington by name, I can only assume that he saw him as a real threat. The bunker was full of whiteboards and boxes of research. I believe he honestly believed his work was in need of protection."

"And the man who worked for Evington did show up at Bek's place," Ape added.

"He did," I acknowledged. "I guess we'll never know if he was just there to talk, or if he was there to force Bek to turn over his work, but his presence at Bek's cabin does seem to indicate that the man had a legitimate reason to fear his work would be compromised."

"So, did he kill this man?" Phoenix asked.

"I'm not sure," I answered. "As I just pointed out, Bek seemed to have had a motive to have done so, but by all appearances, Bek left his property once he'd stored his most sensitive work in the bunker. We've looked at the surveillance recordings, and in the early entries, we can see him moving around the property. And then the day before the first time you all went out and found him gone, the movement just stops. We see Bek head toward the bunker and then nothing. I think it's highly likely that once he'd moved everything he needed to move, he left."

"Left to go where?" Chip asked. "His car is still there."

I shrugged. "At this point, I'm going to assume that Bek either hired a car or had a friend pick him up. We didn't find a call to a friend or a car service in his phone records, but the only number we have is the one Skeet gave us. The only calls made to that cell phone were from Skeet. I think it's possible, even likely, that the man had other cell phones."

"Different cell phones for different contacts," Phoenix said.

"Exactly."

"So at this point, all we know is that someone shot and killed the man from the yacht when he went to visit Bek and that Skeet, thinking Bek was the killer, moved the body."

I nodded. "That about sums it up. A woman named Penelope Dario is in jail for the murder of her ex-husband, Braylon Dario, which is why Skeet decided he needed to speak up rather than keeping what he knew to himself any longer."

"But he is okay, right?" Phoenix asked.

I nodded again. "Skeet is with Adam Winchester. Adam has taken over as temporary custodian, and Skeet is staying at his house for the time being."

"Lucky guy," Ape said. "I'd like to get a look inside that place. Do you think if I get arrested, Winchester will let me stay with him as well?"

I laughed. "I think there are easier ways to get a peek inside the house. Currently, the attorney who is representing Skeet doesn't want him talking to anyone, but once that restriction is lifted, I'm sure Adam will be happy to have you all over for a visit."

"He did seem like a nice guy when we met him the other day," Cosmo said.

"He is a nice guy, and he really likes teens. At this point, I'm going to suggest you all keep a low profile until this is all sorted out. I know you have zombie duty later this evening. I'll call you tomorrow and let you know if there have been any updates."

Once the kids left for the community center, I called Adam back to see if he'd heard from Carson. He reported that he had and that Carson was trying to get me in to see Penelope around four and said he'd call me back to confirm.

In the meantime, I decided to see if I could figure out where Bek might have gone if he'd left voluntarily. I didn't really know the man well enough to know who he would reach out to for help, but the man had lived in Seattle for a long time. Bek must have developed relationships during his tenure at the local university. Maybe he'd reached out to a fellow professor or even a student. The problem at this point was that there were too many possibilities. I needed to narrow things down a bit.

I was just about to call Adam back again when he called me to let me know that Carson had arranged for me to meet with Penelope at four as I hoped. The visit would be fifteen minutes and only fifteen minutes, and our conversation would be recorded. That was fine with me. I had nothing to hide. I didn't think Penelope did either.

"Before you go," I said to Adam. "If Skeet is there, can you ask him who he thinks Bek would reach out to if he wanted to go into hiding but needed help?"

Adam asked me to hold while he talked to Skeet. A minute later, he came back on the line and informed me that it was Skeet's opinion that if Bek needed help that he couldn't get locally, he might ask a woman named Mariah Stallman. Mariah had been a student when Bek worked for the university in Seattle, and the two had gotten along fabulously. In fact, as far as Skeet knew, Mariah was the only one from his old life Bek stayed in touch with. I asked

Adam to ask Skeet if he knew how to contact Mariah. Skeet did but preferred to do it himself. I knew Skeet wasn't supposed to be interacting with others, but Adam assured me he'd actually make the call, and then he'd call me back and share what he'd found.

I agreed to the plan since it seemed evident at this point that if Evington had sent Dario to speak to Bek, then Evington didn't have Bek, as the Geek Squad initially thought he had.

After I hung up, I glanced at the clock. I still had an hour before I needed to head over to the jail to talk to Penelope, and I felt like I'd done what I could regarding the case of the missing professor unless a new clue came to light, so I decided to take a short walk down the boardwalk. I hadn't gotten my run in that morning and was feeling a little stiff. Hopefully, I'd be able to return to my regular schedule tomorrow.

When I returned to my office, I had a message from Adam to call him.

"Hey, Adam. Did you get ahold of Mariah Stallman?"

"I did. As it turns out, Mariah is the one who picked Bek up Friday afternoon. He'd arranged to meet her in the parking area near the cabin. I guess Bek decided to take a last-minute trip to Switzerland and didn't want to leave his car at the airport, so he asked Mariah, who lives in Seattle, to come and get him and then drop him at the airport. She said she did as he asked but really doesn't specifically know where Bek might have gone off to. He's supposed to call her when he returns from his trip if he needs another ride."

"Does she have a way to get ahold of him?" I asked. It would be helpful if we could verify that he actually had been in Switzerland this entire time.

"Mariah said she knew a few people she could check with," Adam informed me. "I'll call you when I hear back from her, but if Bek has been overseas since before Dario came to town, then he couldn't have been the one to kill him."

"Yeah, it's beginning to look like Bek isn't our guy. I have my face-to-face with Penelope in thirty minutes. Maybe she knows something she isn't saying. I really am hoping that we'll have a better lead to follow up on once I'm able to find out what she knows."

"Call me when your visit is over."

"I will. Todd didn't give me long, so it won't be late."

I almost expected Todd to change his mind and deny my visit once I'd arrived, but instead, he greeted me with a smile before taking me into a room I suspected was primarily used for interrogations. Penelope was already in the room when I arrived. She was cuffed, which I felt was completely unnecessary, but I didn't want to rock the boat and get kicked out, so I didn't say anything.

"Hi, Penelope. My name is Ainsley Holloway," I began once I'd taken a seat.

"I know who you are. You're friends with Josie and Tegan."

"That's right. I'm also a private investigator and have been asked by Josie to try to figure out what actually happened on the day Braylon Dario died."

"I didn't shoot him," she said.

"I believe you. The main focus of my investigation is to figure out who did. It occurred to me that you might have some ideas about that."

"Ideas?"

"As to who killed Braylon. I know you ran after your husband beat you. I know you've been in hiding and only recently showed up here in Gooseberry Bay. Is it your opinion that Braylon knew you were here?"

"When I saw him, I thought he'd found me, but then after having a chance to think about it, I realized that there was no way he could know where I was. I hadn't told anyone. Not another living soul. And I changed my look quite a lot. My hair is different, I wear colored contacts, and I dress differently. Everything about Anne Jorgenson is different than Penelope Dario."

"So why do you think he was here if not to try to track you down?" I knew the answer to this, but I was interested in what she knew.

"That new attorney, Carson, told me that Braylon was here to talk to a man named Ivan Beklund on Ronald Evington's behalf. That makes sense. He came in Evington's yacht, and I know that the firm Braylon worked for does jobs for Evington sometimes. The fact that he just happened to wander into the very bar and grill where I work is both terrifying and an amazing coincidence, but it's starting to look as if that was the case."

"I understand that when you saw Braylon, you ran and hid in the woods."

"That's right. I stayed there all night. Until it started to get light. I was going to run again and was on my way to my place to get my things, but I noticed that the yacht was gone. If the yacht was gone, then maybe Braylon was gone. I really wanted to stay here in Gooseberry Bay, so I decided to clean up, show up at work, and see what I could find out. If Braylon hadn't been asking around about me, if he hadn't been showing folks my photo and asking if they'd seen me, then maybe he really had been here for some other reason, and I wouldn't have to run."

"And then?"

"And then Deputy Todd arrested me for killing Braylon. I'm glad he's dead, but I didn't do it. I swear."

I paused, gathered my thoughts, and then continued. "I believe that you didn't kill Braylon, but someone did. Do you have any idea who that someone might be?"

She narrowed her gaze and wrinkled her brow. "Braylon had a lot of enemies. I heard someone saying that it was the man he was here to see who killed him."

"That was a theory at one point, but it turns out the man Braylon was here to see is out of the country. Can you think of anyone else? Maybe someone aware of your story who wanted to protect you."

"No one knows my story. At least no one did before this whole thing happened. Braylon made sure he kept me under lock and key when I had bruises in need of healing. And no matter how bad I was hurt, he never let me go to the hospital. I really can't think of anyone who would kill him for what he did to me."

"What about someone on the yacht. There was a man who came to town a few hours after Braylon. Could someone from the yacht have wanted him dead?"

She frowned, and then her eyes grew large.

"You thought of something."

"Nothing that I know for sure."

"That's okay," I persuaded. "Just tell me what occurred to you."

She looked uncertain, but eventually, she spoke. "I guess you know that Braylon was a partner in a large firm. What you might not know is that he only made partner about five years ago. He'd been in contention for the position with another man, Xavier Saulsman. Both men had been with the law firm for almost their entire careers, and both men had worked hard to make partner. When it was decided that there was only one partnership available, the two men became fierce competitors."

"So Braylon won, and it's your opinion that this other man was a sore loser and would have reason to want him dead."

She shook her head. "He didn't win. Not really. He cheated. Braylon made a mistake, a huge one that cost the firm an important client. Braylon knew the error would cost him the partnership, so he somehow fixed things to make it look like the error was Xavier's fault. Xavier tried to defend himself, but Braylon was convincing, so Braylon got the coveted position, and Xavier was fired."

What a jerk, I thought to myself. "I can understand why you might think this Xavier had reason to want Braylon dead, but why now?"

"Xavier went to work for Evington after he was fired. Mr. Evington has this huge company, and he has an in-house legal staff as well as attorneys on retainer. Those who work directly for Evington mostly take care of paperwork: contracts, patents, that sort of thing. If there is something juicier going on, Evington will use one of the high-dollar firms he has an agreement with. Given the fact that Braylon arrived on Evington's yacht, I'm going to assume he was in town on Evington's behalf. If he was, then it seems possible that Evington might have sent one of his staff attorneys as well, especially if Braylon was supposed to convince the man he was here to meet to sign a contract of some sort."

Suddenly, Penelope's story made sense. If Dario and Saulsman had both been sent to deal with Beklund, then perhaps Saulsman had seen their partnership as an opportunity to get his revenge.

Based on what I knew about Dario's personality, I was willing to bet that Dario may have even egged him on during the ride over.

Of course, this was only a theory, and proof would be needed, so I called Deputy Todd in and had Penelope go over her story once again. I half figured Todd would brush her story off as an attempt to gain her freedom, but for some reason, he seemed to believe she might be onto something. He asked about Saulsman's overall build, which seemed odd until I realized someone else had seen a man fitting that description walking through town with a gun in his waistband.

Since the interview was basically over, I was escorted out. I guessed at this point, I'd just have to count on Todd to follow up. It was his job to do so, and he had seemed interested in getting the story, but during the year that I'd lived in Gooseberry Bay, I'd realized that Todd was only interested in those cases that benefited him in some way.

Deciding to head back to the peninsula, I called Adam and told him what had occurred and then promised to call with an update if anything came from Todd's assurance that he'd look into things. I figured that once I got home, I'd call Parker with an update. Then I'd head over to Jemma and Josie's cottage to fill them in. If everything went as I hoped, Penelope should be freed by the end of the day.

Chapter 16

"Wow, good job, Ainsley." Josie put her hand up for a high five.

"I didn't really do anything other than ask the right questions, but I'm happy everything worked out."

Josie grinned. "Parker called and said that Penelope should be out within the next hour or so. She's going to take her out for a meal and then drop her off at her apartment. I'm sure she must feel relieved now that she no longer has a reason to run."

"Do you think she'll stay here in town?" I asked.

Josie shrugged. "Maybe. She likes it here, but with her ex-husband dead and her need to hide gone, I can see her doing something else. She wasn't actually divorced from Braylon, and it does appear she had a good reason to run, so I'd be willing to bet she'll come out of this with a nice financial settlement of some sort. Once she has that, I guess she can do whatever she wants."

"I still can't believe that Saulsman confessed when the Seattle P.D. picked him up."

"He said he'd always liked Penelope and felt sorry for her. He didn't want her to go to jail for something he'd done," I said. "The man admitted that Dario had been goading him from the moment they both arrived at the yacht. Saulsman said he realized after he killed the guy that he'd overreacted, but the man had ruined his life, and the rage had been building."

Coop came in through the back door. He hadn't been around for a while, and it seemed like it had been at least a week since I'd seen him. Josie got him a beer and invited him to stay for dinner. She had lasagna in the oven that smelled heavenly. I asked Coop about his most recent charter, and he caught us up on life in his world. He had an old army buddy coming for a visit, and I could see that he was nervous about that for some reason. Josie and Jemma both offered to help entertain the man since that was, after all, what friends did.

"So, what's going on with your case?" Coop asked me.

I filled him in, including the information that Bek had been found in Switzerland and was just fine. He wasn't the sort of man who was used to worrying about others or having them worry about him, so he never even considered letting anyone know what he was doing.

I think Skeet realized he might have overreacted, but despite the fact that Skeet would still have to go to court for moving the body, things seemed to have worked out. Carson was trying to make sure Skeet's sentence included community service but no jail time, and Adam had made plans to allow Skeet to live with him until he could be legally emancipated.

"It sure does seem that you girls get pulled into pretty much every weird thing that goes on in these parts," Coop said.

"We're women and not girls," Jemma corrected in a tone that sounded an awful lot like scolding. "And we pay attention. It's not so much that we get pulled into events in our environment. It's more that we have an opinion and intentionally step in to solve the crimes in this town that Deputy Todd and his merry band of men are unable to."

Coop smiled and winked at Jemma, who blushed. Could there be something going on between the two? I'd never heard either refer to their friendship as anything more than just that, but there was no denying that Coop had found Jemma's outburst adorable.

"So who's hungry?" Josie asked, coming to Jemma's rescue.

We all agreed that we were and sat down to eat. As we ate, the conversation segued into topics relating to the weeks and months ahead. With the holiday season upon us, there were plans to make and events to attend. I knew that Coop had never attended the Winter Ball. Last year, Jemma and I had gone together. But this year, Jemma jumped right in and asked him to attend with her. I figured he'd politely bow out, so I was shocked when he responded that he'd think about it.

Coop and Jemma. Who would have thought. I knew Coop had a past that continued to color his present and hoped Jemma didn't end up getting hurt, but when I looked at the two of them and thought about what great people they both were, I realized they'd likely make a go of it despite whatever challenges might lay ahead.

Chapter 17

"I can't believe you have this in your home," Cosmo said to Adam as he literally drooled over the Winchester telescope. "There are observatories that don't have a telescope as good as this one."

"My father was into astronomy. He built this room at the top of the house specifically to house the telescope."

"You should see the computer lab," Chip said, wandering in with Skeet, who'd taken him to see it. "Talk about state-of-the-art equipment. When I walked in, I figured I'd died and gone to heaven."

"I like the game room best, but it's all cool," Skeet said. "I can't believe I get to live here. At least for now."

"And I'm happy to have you," Adam said. "It gets lonely rambling around this big ol' house. It's so quiet."

Phoenix laughed. "I can be noisy. Trust me. If you need company, just call. I'd love to try out that gourmet kitchen."

"Any time," Adam smiled.

I had to admit that Adam really did look happy. He'd been talking about filling his big old house with teenagers. I don't think that this was exactly what he'd planned, but he seemed really happy about the way things had turned out, at least in the short term.

I'd intended to spend the day working on my search for Avery with Adam, but when I'd mentioned that I'd planned to spend the day at the house on Piney Point to the Geek Squad members, they all asked if they could come along to check on Skeet. I'd called Adam, who'd talked to Carson, who'd indicated that it would be okay to let the friends spend time together now that the legal case was close to being resolved. Adam had offered to act as guardian for Skeet, but I had a feeling that Skeet came with a package. In a way, I supposed that the entire Geek Squad would benefit from their acquaintance with Adam, and in the long run, I really believed that Adam would benefit from spending time with teens such as those he planned to help with his foundation. After only a few days with Skeet, he'd already reconsidered a few of the things he'd been thinking.

"You know, every secret society needs a place to meet," Ape said, "A bat cave of sorts. Maybe this should be ours."

Skeet looked at Adam, who shrugged. "Fine by me, but you clean up after yourselves and stay out of the wine cellar."

Skeet and Ape high-fived each other after promising to be ideal guests whenever the gang got together. I hoped Adam didn't regret his decision to open his home to these five socially awkward geniuses, but they seemed like good kids and not the sort to really create any problems.

"Who's up for pizza?" Adam asked.

All the kids agreed they were. I figured Adam intended to get takeout, but as it turned out, Adam has his own brick pizza oven and promised to teach everyone how to make their own.

"You got a good guy there," Phoenix said to me as all the guys headed toward the kitchen.

"Oh, he's not my guy. Just a friend."

She raised a brow.

"Really," I said with more conviction.

"I have eyes you know. I see the way he watches you when you're otherwise occupied and not paying attention. The man is smitten. Now, I'm not an expert on love, but if I were you, I wouldn't throw that one back."

I was about to argue again that Adam and I really were just friends but hesitated. I supposed there had been times in the past when I'd sensed a bit of chemistry, but we were both busy people, and whatever mutual attraction we shared had never gone anywhere. Still, there were indications that Phoenix might be onto something. Adam had always been there for me. He seemed almost as committed to finding Avery as I was. And then there was that moment at the Winter Ball last year when we'd danced and time had all but stood still. Had it been almost a year since that magical moment?

"We should catch up with the others," I said.

Phoenix looped her arm through mine and started walking. "So about this Winter Ball I've been hearing about," she said. "What exactly do you think it would take to get an invite?"

"Probably not a lot. I'll mention that you'd like to attend to Adam. It seems the event is open to most everyone the brothers know and consider to be a friend."

She turned and grinned at me. "Really?"

I nodded. "Really."

"I'll need a dress."

"Last year, a group of us went to Seattle for dresses. I'm sure we'll have room for one more."

Phoenix screeched as she jumped up and down in a very unladylike manner. "You rock, Ainsley Holloway." She hugged me. "Watch out world," she said in a strong voice. "This geeky girl is about to transform into a princess."

USA Today best-selling author Kathi Daley lives in beautiful Lake Tahoe with her husband, Ken. When she isn't writing, she likes spending time hiking the miles of desolate trails surrounding her home. Find out more about her books at www.kathidaley.com

Made in the USA
Coppell, TX
16 September 2021

62375880R00109